A Dark Genesis

Cheryl Lawson

Also by the author:

Fiction:

The Rubicon Saga
We Are Mars
Storm At Dawn
Break the Dark

Journey to Vega Novellas
Erebus

Anthologies:

Worlds. Dark Drabbles #1 (Black Hare Press)
VSS365 (2019)

First Published in Canada, 2021.
Published by SW Sci-Fi, an imprint of Southernwood Technologies Inc. 2021.

ISBN 978-1-989872-04-8

Dedication

To David and James

ONE

Time log: Year 2185 (Present Day)
Day: 36,135. Hour: 11:22

The noise started as a low reverberation and increased in intensity until all the equipment in the lab rattled on desks and in cabinets.

"That can't be good."

"Oh, Sage. You're always looking for problems where none exist. It's probably just an engine burn for a routine course change."

Sage shot a sideways glance at her supervisor, Lieutenant Mara Quinn, Chief Science Officer.

"Since when does engine ignition make the whole ship shudder?" she asked. Had she even been alive the last time the *Vega Four* did a burn to keep the behemoth ship on its course to the distant Vega star system?

A moment later, the lighting changed from the usual soothing off-white ambience to an alarming red.

"ALERT! ALERT! All hands, brace!"

Gooseflesh crawled up Sage's arms and she said,

"See, Mara. I—"

"Just don't!" Mara glared at her. "No one likes a smartass, trouble-stirrer."

Sage snapped her mouth shut. Her supervisor's reprimand stung but didn't surprise her. She'd been rebuked many times for her strident discontent. Tamping down resentment, she obeyed Mara's instructions to staff and stowed all her research samples and experiments.

Another shudder passed through the ship and the buzz of voices in the lab became a din. Moments later, the bosun's whistle sounded and the room fell silent. Lab workers waited with concerned expressions for the captain's announcement.

Sage shrugged to release the tension in her shoulders. Her discomfort had little to do with the six hours she'd been hunched over, logging results from her latest crop rotation experiments. Soil samples full of microorganisms had been forgotten the instant the alert sounded.

The ship vibrated a third time before the captain's voice echoed over the ship-wide comm.

"Attention crew and passengers, Captain Ellis, here. The command crew and I would like to apologize for the current discomfort you're experiencing. We are traversing an asteroid cloud with objects of significant size. Some direct impact shockwaves against the bow's shield array may be felt. Please do not panic."

Sage knew she should relax, but the announcement only worried her more.

"The time remaining until we are free of the—"

A deafening explosion cut off the captain's voice and a heavy shudder knocked everyone off their feet. Sage floated away from the deck. The gravitational systems were offline and disorienting dizziness threatened to dislodge her breakfast. Sage gulped against the surging discomfort. Then, with almost no time to process the loss of gravity, the ship's systems rebooted, jerking her down to the floor.

"Oof!" Winded, sick and dizzy, she looked around. "What the hell?"

The bosun's whistle sounded again, followed by a strident alarm. The red light began to blink steadily, bathing the lab in bright reds interspersed with bursts of deep maroon.

Something terrible has happened, thought Sage, anxious and still struggling to catch her breath.

"Attention! All crew, general quarters! All passengers assemble at designated emergency shelters and report in. Protocol Alpha. Protocol Alpha."

"Mara?" Sage dragged herself to her feet and searched for the science officer. Her knees throbbed. She sucked in a breath, rubbed the bruises, and hobbled around her bench.

Mara was leaning against a wall. She cradled her head and blood oozed between her fingers.

"You're hurt. Are you able to get up?"

Mara looked dazed and shook her head slowly. Sage helped her stand and guided her to the lab exit. The rest of the technicians and assistants were out in the narrow corridor, waiting for instructions.

Sage checked Mara. In her current condition, the woman would not be able to coordinate the lab's evacuation to the emergency assembly point. The blow to her head seemed to have stunned her.

Taking charge, Sage raised her voice and said, "All right, everyone who's able to walk unaided, make your way to the Deck Six assembly area. Please assist anyone who looks like they might need help. We have to be quick, so let's go, people."

The lab workers shuffled down the corridor. Sage caught the attention of one of her coworkers in the rear.

"Hey Tom, could you help me with Mara? I've got to close up the lab."

"Sure. Want me to wait for you?"

"No. I'll only be a minute. Go ahead and get her seen to."

Sage draped Mara's arm over the young man's shoulders and went back to initiate the lab's emergency shutdown. She collected Mara's device from her desk and jogged out of the lab. The door slid closed behind her. She was relieved when she caught up to the group again. With her imagination running wild, she tried not to panic.

She hated feeling that the ship had somehow been threatened. Their population had ballooned. There weren't enough lifepods to accommodate everyone if an evacuation became necessary and even if the pods were jettisoned safely, there was no telling how long they would be adrift before they were rescued. The sister ships of the *Vega Four* were months away, possibly more. When Ark-Class ships like this one experienced a catastrophe, it was understood that the occupants had only themselves to rely on.

It's irrational stupidity to launch flying cities into deep space, to fend for themselves for who knows how long. Her throat tightened and she blinked back tears. *I didn't choose this life—a "canned" life on a damn generation ship—yet here I am.*

The hundred-year-old *Vega Four* was her entire

world—from cradle to coffin. The thought sent a shiver crawling over her scalp and she forced her thoughts back to her duties. The group had reached their designated assembly point.

She made her way through the gathering throng—other groups were joining theirs—to crouch next to Mara whose headwound had been bandaged.

"Mara, are you okay?"

"I'm fine now, thank you. Bashed my head on the underside of my bench when the gravity fritzed." She gave Sage a shaky smile. "Is that my device?"

Sage handed her the tablet and Mara swiped through the emergency assembly protocols, counting off individuals and listing injuries. When she was done, she read the captain's report and her expression darkened.

"Look at this."

Sage read the brief report.

Her eyes widened. "God! An asteroid got through the array and actually struck the ship?" Myriad implications came to mind. "Are we still on course?"

"It's too soon to see a course deviation," Mara said. "The ship takes weeks to complete single course adjustments. It will be a few days before we know anything conclusive."

"I suppose they have all the time in the universe to put us back on track." Sage huffed, her resentment bubbling to the surface. "Not as if it matters to us, anyway, does it?"

"Stop. Please." Mara glared at her. "My head hurts too much for your fatalism today. Can you just find a crew member and get a status report and action plan for us? I don't want to be sitting out here all day."

Sage stepped around people seated in the shelter and went down the corridor in search of an evacuation coordinator.

Thankfully, that incessant wailing of the alarms has stopped. The crew must have taken care of whatever immediate problems the strike caused.

Guilt washed over Sage as an uncomfortable realization struck. She was enjoying the deviation from routine and mundanity. This eventful day was the most fun she'd had since she finished school four years ago.

Sage wondered for the thousandth time how the original travelers could have done it.

How could they choose to doom their children and grandchildren to this confined and uninspired life? A predetermined life is a tragedy.

She firmly believed in the right to choose your life's path. But this ship robbed the occupants of that choice and removed their self-determination over the most important human right—survival.

TWO

Time log: Day: 36,135. Hour: 16:55

Sage glanced from one face to the next. The lab's afternoon round-up had concluded with nothing more interesting than soil quality reports.

Two hours after the asteroid strike, everyone except the engineers working on the hull, had been sent back to work as if nothing had happened. The Sciences staff had returned to their lab and tidied up, then resumed their tasks.

Sage grappled with everyone's apparent refusal to acknowledge the magnitude of the asteroid strike. Her nerves were still jangled. Resentment burned hot and uncomfortable in her gut. How could everyone brush such a dramatic event aside as if it had been nothing serious? But Sage knew stirring them up would only land her in more trouble with Mara, so she suppressed the urge to yell, growing more impatient as the afternoon dragged on.

She was relieved when her workstation signaled

the end of her shift. With single-minded purpose, she wound her way through the crowded concourse and down into the residential quarters of the ship. Her cabin was the one place she could let off some steam in private.

"Hey, Sage," someone called after her, "are you coming—"

"Nope."

"You okay, girl?"

"Nope."

Without explanation or apology, she kept walking. Her expression was fierce. So much so that everyone moved aside to let her by.

The narrow confines of the single juniors' zone only slowed her marginally. A door slid open on her approach and Sage stepped into the cramped cabin she shared with two roommates. The end of the dayshift meant the privacy of the small compartment would be fleeting.

Stopping just inside the door, she clasped her hands together and seethed through gritted teeth.

"Damn, damn, damn!"

A wall-mounted computer console came to life, blinked with three demerits and her name, and spat out the fines on thin, blue slips of paper.

"Foul language and displays of temper are not permissible. Please take your fines and make an appointment with a duty officer to discuss your infractions." Sage pulled a face at the indifferent voice of the etiquette AI.

The behavior protocols annoyed everyone, but they worked. They prevented altercations that could lead to serious arguments, injury, or death. The inhabitants of _Vega Four_ were policed around the clock. Peace predominated because people self-regulated most of their behavior. Only in serious cases did an arbitration panel convene. If their intervention failed, a few nights in the brig on minimal rations, usually cooled tempers.

Sage had long believed they were also drugged into submission. It was one of those ethical issues she had tried and failed to get an explanation for.

"Screw you," she said to the console, which duly added two more demerits and blue slips.

"I'm so tired of having my emotions capped at boring to cooperative." Her sarcasm was lost on the console. She screamed into her pillow, biting at the cover until a small rip opened in the fabric.

Nanoparticles self-repaired the small hole. Every part of the ship was engineered to maintain the status quo and it drove her mad. Out of sync and constantly at war with the system, Sage's frustration grew daily.

"And no one seems to care that we just ran into space rocks. No one!"

Only hours after the incident, the running news tickers displayed nothing about the asteroids.

Perhaps it's a deliberate cover-up. More likely nobody thinks it's of any consequence. So why do I?

Her distrust of the information vacuum made her wary. The most exciting and unbelievable thing had happened and everyone else seemed to have already forgotten about it.

"In my opinion, that's a mistake," she muttered.

"Who are you talking to, Sage?"

One of her roommates, Ash, stood in the doorway of the cabin, frowning at her.

"You know me—just myself, as usual."

Ash, tall and aloof, almost cracked a smile. Nudging past Sage, she changed into a clean shirt and pants.

"Hot date?" Sage cringed inwardly. Her awkwardness at Ash's unexpected appearance while she sulked made her say the first lame thing that came to mind.

"Seriously? A hot date? No one talks like that anymore." Ash sneered. "It's the Twenty-second century, Sage, not 2059."

"God! I'm sorry I'm being weird. The asteroid strike rattled me."

"I guess it was something different, but it didn't bother me." Ash combed her hair and showed no interest in talking about the asteroid.

"Well, I think it's strange and wrong that no one's talking about it. Why am I the only one who's freaked out by what happened?"

"You freak out at everything." Ash shut the locker. "What *would* be strange is to think the strike *is* a big deal when it isn't. If the cap says nothing, we carry on. What else can we do? Relax, Sage. Or don't—whatever. Now, let me by so that I can at least go unwind. It's been a long day."

Ash pushed past her and left. The stink of her disapproval mingled with the scent of her fresh application of deodorant.

Sage wished desperately for the same casually dismissive attitude. *Why can't I let it go? Why can't I ever let it go? What's wrong with me?*

"Damn and f-f-f—" Sage stopped short as the console lit up again.

THREE

Time log: Day: 36,135. Hour: 18:07

"How's it looking, Noah?"

"The control panel cover is destroyed, so I'm guessing it's also gonna be messed up inside."

"Copy that. Proceed to panel cover removal and internal systems diagnostic."

"Copy." Noah reached a thick, padded glove towards the tool bag held against the hull with its own magnetic field. A breath of warm air licked down his back and he blinked, momentarily distracted by the activity inside his suit. He had only ever done two extra-vehicular walks.

This third EV walk was different.

The scale of the damage done by the asteroid was jaw-dropping. The jagged scrapes and tears down the length of the main section's outer hull suggested a shallow glancing blow by something massive. Noah struggled to keep his imagination in check. A more direct hit would have been devastating.

"Mike says that rock was twice the size of the ship. I don't understand how the command crew could have missed it," Noah's partner, Trigg, muttered as they worked. They were on a suit-to-suit channel to keep the main channel clear for team-related comms.

"Well, I heard it ricocheted off another asteroid and changed trajectory last minute. The change came too late for nav con to take evasive maneuvers." Noah couldn't see Trigg's face, but he sensed her glaring at him. "Maybe let's cut those folks some slack, Trigg."

"Jesus Christ, you do realize no one else can actually hear you sucking up right now."

"I see you're not wasting this EVA, either." Noah chuckled, accustomed to Trigg's jibes. Her competence made up for her abrasive personality and the trouble she attracted onboard. There was no one else he trusted more to be his engineering partner.

"Just shut up and get that cov—ow!" Trigg jerked and the safety tether between the two suits snapped taut. "Shit! Something just hit me. Suit's losing pressure and venting atmosphere." She cartwheeled away from the ship.

The tether dragged Noah around and he grabbed a handle near his tool bag to stop from being pulled into an uncontrolled drift along with Trigg.

"Shit! Hold on." He wound his free arm around the line, gave it a gentle tug to stop her spin and gathered her back in towards the ship with care. His HUD lit up, displaying Trigg's suit issues and vital statistics, which were falling rapidly. He switched to main comms. "We have a problem, Bo. Trigg's suit is compromised and isn't self-repairing. We're coming back in."

"Copy that. I have her stats. You have two minutes until her suit goes critical. Move."

"Copy."

Trigg's visor had already started to fog up. Her eyes were saucers of panic. Noah gave two short tugs on the tether to guide her past him and Trigg grabbed a handle on the other side of the tool bag. She dragged herself against the hull with a dull thud.

"Let's go. Can you see the airlock?"

"No. My visor's fogged."

"Shit. Okay. I'm going around you and I'm going to guide you in. Keep a hand on the tether, the other on the handrail." Noah pushed past her. The sound their suits rubbing together reached his helmet as muted squeaks and scuffs, but he could barely hear it over his heavy breathing. His heart raced and his mouth was dry.

A light tug on the tether caused him to stop.

"What is it, Trigg? Are you okay?"

"Your tools. Don't leave them out here." Her suggestion seemed out of place, but he knew what she meant.

If he left his tools outside, the bag would freeze to the hull. He'd have a hell of a time retrieving it and the precious, difficult-to-replace tools would be lost, fused together permanently by the frigid coldness of space.

"Give me one sec." He reached past Trigg and gave the bag a hard yank. It didn't budge. "Shit." Noah braced his boots against the hull and pulled again. When the bag suddenly came loose, its weight and trajectory nearly sent him into a tumble. The line snapped taut a second time and Trigg grunted in his ear.

"Are you done messing around with your fucking bag, Noah?" She reeled him back in.

"Sorry, Trigg. I forgot to demagnetize it. Let's go."

They shuffled along the length of the tether as quickly as their clumsy suits allowed.

"I'm almost out of air. You'll have to do the hatch cover." Trigg's teeth chattered. Her visor was opaque. If the condensation from her rapidly cooling suit got any worse, wet electrical circuits could short-circuit and shut her suit down.

"Hang on, okay? Almost there."

Noah turned the wheel on the airlock hatch and

the cover swung open. He grabbed Trigg and shoved her through the opening, then disconnected the safety tether and pulled himself in. Once inside the airlock, he spun the wheel and sealed the hatch.

"Now—repressurize now, Bo!"

Trigg lay in a heap on the deck of the airlock. The intense UV decontamination lamps glowed blue. The light crawled over their suits. Noah helped Trigg turn over so the rest of her suit could be cleaned. He stood and shuffled in a slow circle until the light changed back to green. Trigg sat up, slid her helmet locks open and yanked it off.

She sucked in a breath and coughed. Her face was damp and pale. Her body trembled from shock. Noah took off his helmet and knelt beside her.

"Are you okay?"

"I'll be fine. My arm hurts like a b—" She hissed and squeezed her eyes closed.

He helped her stand and dismantle her suit. When he removed the left arm, she yelped and sank back to the floor.

A puncture wound the size of a pea, with ragged, burned edges oozed blood down to her elbow.

"I need to lift your arm to check if it's gone all the way through. Ready?"

She nodded and winced.

He studied the underside of her arm. There was no exit wound. "The good news is, whatever hit you was very hot and cauterized the flesh on its way in, so there's not too much bleeding." He smiled encouragingly. "Let's get you to the infirmary."

He put an arm around Trigg's waist and lifted her to her feet. They cleared the airlock and were met with applause from the engineering crew in the external operations control room. The chief engineer, Bo Nash, waited at the top of the stairs near the airlock door.

"Trigg!"

Bo had been watching them anxiously through the airlock's observation window.

"She'll be okay. We think a micro meteor hit her," Noah said. "It burned right through her suit and embedded in her arm."

"Doctor Mills," Bo said over comms to the on-duty physician in the infirmary. "That injured crew member is on their way to you now."

Noah guided Trigg carefully down the ship's narrow passages and helped her step over bulkheads. He stooped as they traversed the tight spaces, ducking to miss low fixtures and bulkhead frames. Ever since he'd turned sixteen, he'd been too tall for most of the corridors and gangways of *Vega Four*. Like his father, he towered over most people. In contrast to his size, or perhaps to make up for it, he had a very agreeable personality. Everyone liked him, and he generally had no problem with anyone.

Except for Sage Lang. Noah had a hard time resolving his feelings around the brittle friendship they'd shared since school. From an early age, she had intrigued him. She'd also pestered him, irritated him and, on occasion, sulked at him. He reluctantly maintained their friendship hoping her behavior would soften as they matured. Lately however, he'd needed to distance himself from her. Sage was heading for a major clash with authority, and he didn't want to be the one left picking up all the pieces. He was tired of being the dutiful friend in the midst of her crises. He preferred a peaceful life. Sage was an agent of chaos and tension. He reminded himself of this once again as he dismissed a call from her.

Third one today. I know what you're up to, Sage, and it's not going to work. But it was a lie. He knew she'd get under his skin sooner or later. She always did.

Trigg passed out a few paces from the ship's infirmary. She slumped against Noah's side and his muscles protested the unexpected load. He half-carried, half-dragged her over the threshold then hoisted her gently onto an exam table. A moment later, medical staff swarmed around the unconscious woman and he retreated to the waiting room. Bo had followed them down to the infirmary and spoke to the admissions person at the main desk.

"Upper left arm," Noah heard him say. "She should probably also be examined for pressure-loss trauma." Bo swiped through files on his device and attached the video file of the EVA to the admissions intake device, then took a seat next to Noah.

"It might be a while. We should go eat something," he said.

"I'm not hungry." Worried about his friend and partner, Noah couldn't eat. Why had Trigg fainted? The wound had not appeared to be much more than a deep puncture. She'd sustained worse in a more serious accident about six months ago. That time, she'd walked to the infirmary on a broken ankle.

"Well, I can get something for you and Trigg to eat later."

"Go get some dinner, Bo. We're okay. I'll wait for Trigg and we'll get a sandwich after she's discharged. I'm sure she won't be that long. It looked like it was just a cut."

"Right. I'll see you back at work then. Tell Trigg to take the rest of the shift off, would ya?"

"Thanks, Bo."

The chief left and Noah took out his device. He watched the playback of the incident and couldn't even see the meteor before it struck Trigg's suit. The only physical evidence was the sudden appearance of a vapor trail from a dark hole in her suit's sleeve.

There had been hundreds, if not thousands, of EVAs in the past ninety-nine years. As far as he knew, this was the first time a crew member had been struck by anything during a spacewalk.

He sat back and closed his eyes, relief at their narrow escape overwhelming him. A fatigue like he'd never known settled on him and he fought the urge to fall asleep.

"Noah?"

"Trigg." He blinked and rose. "How are you feeling?"

"A bit beat up. That whole incident was just so weird."

"Tell me about it. At least you get to go down in history. You'll be famous now."

"You mean, infamous, don't you? The first crew member to be hit by space junk." Trigg tried to smile, but her expression betrayed her shock.

"Hey, you've been through worse."

"I'll be okay." Trigg sniffed. "The suit venting scared me, though. I've never had that happen for real. I mean, we're trained to handle it, but that's not the same. You can always call it quits on a sim. You can't call it quits when your suit's leaking for real and you can't see a fu—" She rolled her eyes. "... anything."

"I can only guess how scary it must have been. But you stayed calm, and we got you back in with no issues."

"Thanks, Noah. You saved my life."

"I didn't do much. Apart from me forgetting my toolkit, the situation was completely under control." He wanted her to feel safe again.

She grinned. "Let's get something to eat and forget about it, okay?"

"Sounds good."

The pair walked out of the infirmary towards the main concourse and their favorite sandwich shop.

Trays in hand, they found a table in the food court and sat down. Trigg winced and shrugged but said nothing.

"Tell me about your arm," Noah said. "What'd the doc say?"

"Well, whatever hit me fused to the bone. Doctor Mills said that unless I choose to do a bone graft to remove it, I should get used to it being there. The scan showed it as a calcium-based mass which means it shouldn't cause any issues."

"Did you get any drugs to help with pain?" Trigg still looked so pale.

"She gave me an antibiotic and analgesic patch to wear for the next few days." She shrugged. "Worst part of it all is there's this intense itching. I don't know how to describe it, but it's like the fragment is shifting around and it burns. It reminds me it's still in there. To say I'm irritated is a fucking understatement."

Noah raised an eyebrow at her cursing.

A demerit slip was smoothly delivered to their table by one of the automated etiquette robots that cruised the concourse. Trigg grabbed the slip and shoved it in a pocket, clearly not worried about the fine. With everything else she'd been through Noah didn't blame her for swearing. Under the circumstances, he didn't think he could do any better.

"Well, I'm sure the discomfort will ease as the wound heals."

"You're right, I know. It's probably all in my head." With a far-off look, she took a sip of her drink. "Do you remember that time a screwdriver head broke off in my foot when I fell down the ladder in the bridge maintenance shaft? That was a fun day."

"Oh Trigg, you really have to stop getting in front of stuff that can stab or shoot holes in you." Noah chuckled and sipped his coffee.

She laughed. "Curse of being an engineer, am I right?"

He was glad to see her smile. They finished their dinner before heading back in the direction of Engineering.

"You're heading back to work? You do know Bo gave you time off to recuperate, right?"

"I'll be fine," she said.

Sometime later, Trigg came over to his workbench to say the pain meds had kicked in and she needed to leave. She said goodbye then trudged out of Engineering.

Noah continued to work long into the night. The ventilation system seemed to be all out of sync—cold in some places, hot in others, and circulation volumes were down across most of the ship. Systems were sufficiently screwed up to require a major repair job, starting with the damage to the hull. Noah suspected a hull breach that was venting atmosphere. It was important to plug the leak and reestablish pressure.

Everything else would come back in line if they could get the pressure balanced again.

He packed up and left at the end of his shift, his thoughts dwelling on the accident. He made a note to check with Bo when the next EVA was scheduled. After Trigg was hit, a drone had been sent out to monitor the debris field. Until he knew they would be safe out there, Bo had postponed EVAs. He didn't want to risk more people being injured.

Down in the crew quarters, Noah hit the showers, then dragged himself back to his cabin and crawled into his bunk, exhausted. He had just fallen asleep when his device buzzed. Squinting in the dim light, he flipped it over to look for the mute function. The device buzzed again, and sleep slipped farther away.

Should I ignore it or answer? Sage has the worst timing!

He opened a drawer in his side table and stowed the buzzing device. He decided sleep was more important than wasting valuable shut-eye on her incessant questions.

He guessed she was still fishing for information about the asteroid strike. It's what she did whenever something unusual happened. The woman was a constant irritant, a bit like the rock in Trigg's arm. He couldn't get rid of her.

Noah sighed heavily and turned over in the narrow bunk, facing the wall. He threw his pillow over his head and squeezed his eyes shut.

He hated to admit it, but there was also a part of him that liked Sage coming to him for answers. He enjoyed being the center of someone's attention. He liked being the center of *her* attention. She didn't know. No one knew how he felt about her. He'd kept it a secret because she always talked to him like a sibling and even treated him like one sometimes. She could be dismissive and abusive. Being friends with Sage was a bit like standing too close to the pulse engine core. You were likely to get burned. He'd had too much to deal with in the past day to worry about that now, and he drifted back to sleep.

Much later, it was the small part of him that liked to be needed by Sage that urged him to watch all of her video messages—twelve in total. It would seem the woman had not slept, and he could understand why. Her latest conspiracy theory was well-developed and disturbing. She'd had a lot of time to think it through. He yawned and stretched. Her final message stripped away the last vestiges of sleep and he got up, determined to cut off her weird scheming and ideas. She'd gone too far this time.

But first things first, Noah. You're gonna be late for work if you don't get your ass in gear.

FOUR

Time log: Day: 36,136. Hour: 11:21

"Look at that. What do you suppose it is?" Bo said. The whole of Engineering was gathered around the monitors displaying the unusual visual.

Noah squinted at the screen. The light on that section of the hull was terrible and the remote camera was not able to show anything other than a smooth, uniform sheen.

"I have no idea, but it wasn't there yesterday." Noah remembered the control panel had been badly damaged, sporting a large, ragged hole through it. What he saw on the monitor today looked crusted-over. There was no sign of the collision damage.

"Did someone else go out there and spray something over the impact area? Could it be some kind of malformed resin?"

"No one's been out there since the EVA Trigg and I did yesterday, and neither of us got a chance to do much more than look the damage over," Noah said.

37

"Strange. Trigg, have you seen this?" Bo shot the question over his shoulder. "And good afternoon. You're late."

"What is it?" She ignored Bo's sarcasm and his reprimand and leaned over to squint at the screen.

"Hey, Trigg." Noah greeted his partner and gave her an appraising look. She looked pale again today. "Are you feeling okay?"

"I didn't sleep well. My arm is killing me. It's all swollen this morning. Look." She gingerly shrugged her arm out of her overall top to reveal the extent of the bruising and swelling. "It goes down past my elbow."

"What the hell? I think you need to head to the infirmary," Bo said, holding out his hand for the demerit slip and pocketing it without blinking.

"Heading there now. I just came in to ask if I can take some time off. I can't do much today, Bo. Sorry."

"No problem. I need you a hundred percent, Trigg. Noah can pick up the slack today."

"Great, thanks." She pulled her sleeve back up and looked at Noah. "I owe you, pal."

"Yeah, you do. Get better. Will I see you at the Sandwich Shack later?" It was a well-established routine of theirs.

"I still need to eat, you big goof." She grinned and

slowly headed out.

"That arm looks terrible. God, I hope she's okay."

Noah nodded. "Sometimes I think they're too quick to discharge us from the infirmary in the name of productivity."

"I hear ya, but this ship won't run itself."

"Or clean itself." They both turned to look at the monitor again.

"Let's do an EVA to assess the residue." Bo divvied up tasks for the spacewalk and was about to send them off when an urgent message came through from Command.

"A ventilation shut-down?" He checked the screens of operational data for the *Vega Four*. "We've got the malfunction showing up, but according to my boards we still have airflow."

"Shit," Noah muttered.

"What is it?"

"There's a rolling shut-down on the container decks, and for some reason, the alarm for that zone only went to the bridge."

"We'll need to get on this quick."

"I'll take Arjun and we can check it out."

"Report ASAP, Noah. The second alarm just blinked on. Looks like we also have a humidity and flow control failure in Section Two."

Noah and his partner for the day, Arjun Reddy, grabbed their tool bags and a backpack of equipment and diagnostic devices. They left Engineering. The mostly empty storage hangars in Section Two were located in the aft of the *Vega Four.* The supplies the bays had been loaded with on Earth had long since been used up.

"How weird is that? It's hot and damp down here," Arjun said.

"The lack of ventilation should make it colder, not hotter. Something's up. It's like that forest yoga studio in the fitness center."

"I wouldn't know. I've never been in there."

Noah glanced at Arjun. Sweat shone on the man's face. Noah felt a trickle roll down his own neck. This was unusual, for sure.

"Ventilation's definitely offline. It's as quiet as the morgue down here, Bo."

"Copy that. Diagnostics as soon as you can, guys. It's starting to feel a little warm up here, too."

"Will do."

Noah opened the door of the engineering works and set up a tripod light facing the big control panel. He wiped his eyes on his sleeve and swore silently at the humidity.

The hangar echoed every sound and the men worked in hushed tones to try and diagnose the problem with the ventilation system.

Arjun dropped a screwdriver and the clatter of it hitting the metal deck reverberated through the huge, empty space.

"This hangar's starting to give me the creeps."

"Same," Noah said and blinked away sweat, trying to focus on quickly completing the diagnostic.

Forty minutes passed and they were no closer to discovering the issue when Arjun straightened to stretch his back.

"Man, this is frustrat—" He stopped. "Hey, what is that? Noah, take a look up there."

Noah followed the direction of Arjun's gaze to the vaulted ceiling.

"Can you make it out?" the other man asked. Their eyes worked to adjust to the gloom in the high corner.

"It looks the same as that crust on the outside of the ship. That's odd." Noah turned the tripod light around and directed the three lamps at the roof. A dull crust had formed over the ceiling conduits and tiles.

Both men stared at haphazard, iridescent protrusions.

"Is that rock?" Arjun scratched his head.

"It looks like it. But it can't be. How did it get there?"

Noah used the lights to follow the smooth, hard growth all the way back to a ventilation fan which stood idle. The rock appeared to have come from the shaft beyond the fan and crystallized on the walls and roof of the hangar. It transformed the corner of the empty space.

"It looks like the caves I remember from our Geology studies at school," Noah said. "But it can't be. What do we have on this ship that could form stalactites?"

"Nothing I know of."

Noah thought for a moment. "Maybe it's some kind of effluent that's solidified—like an antifreeze leak." He was relieved to arrive at some kind of reasonable explanation. A coolant leak seemed like a simple enough fix.

"Maybe, like Trigg's suit, something penetrated the ship and ruptured a tank." Arjun completed the theory.

Noah radioed back to Bo and explained what they'd found.

"That explains why it's a rolling problem. All right. I'm shutting the antifreeze tank valves and switching ventilation to fans only until we know more. Good work. Now, find that leak."

"Yes, sir," Noah replied and smiled at Arjun. He gave the rocky mass one more look and ordered a clean-up crew to the hangar, explaining the problem.

The pair returned to Engineering and climbed down the narrow ladders into the working bowels of the ship. The ventilation factory was two levels below the engineering control room, and it was even hotter and more humid down there. Noah's damp shirt clung to his back. He hunched over.

"I can't even stand up straight down here." His discomfort chipped away at his normally even temper and after close inspection, he hissed with annoyance. Neither of the antifreeze tanks appeared to be damaged. "Damn it. There's nothing malfunctioning down here." He threw his screwdriver back into his bag.

"Control issue. It can only be." Arjun voiced the very thing Noah was thinking.

He nodded and straightened, only to smack his head painfully on a heavy bracket cradling slick, wet pipes.

"Shit!"

"You okay?" Arjun stopped and waited for him.

"I'm fine. But I think we may have found somewhere onboard that the etiquette AI doesn't monitor us."

Arjun grinned. "It's probably too loud in here. Just not today."

Noah looked around at the silent machinery that normally thrummed and pumped out breathable air. He tried to dispel the nagging sense that trouble was around the next corner.

The sweat-soaked men climbed back up the ladder and emerged into the relative coolness of Engineering. Noah wiped his face. He'd never experienced such heat.

"Well, it's not an antifreeze leak. But with the whole system on the fritz, I'm wondering why it's so damn hot still. The ship should be cooling, not heating up."

"Something else must be generating the heat," Bo said.

"Have we checked that the pulse core is operating nominally?" Arjun asked.

"It's not the core. Nothing out of the norm up there. No alarms, no visible issues. I had them check the moment we knew about the heat problem."

"Then maybe there's a latent fire. Something in between the external ice shield and inner hull." Noah worried that the longer they took to nail down the problem and fix it, the slimmer their chances of success were.

"It's a possibility, but there've been no alerts.

I'll get hold of Command. We'll need to run a ship-wide sensor diagnostic. In the meantime, we should scramble the fire teams and start a deck-by-deck sweep with hand-held sensors."

Bo disappeared into the elevator to go in search of the captain. Noah and Arjun sent the call ship-wide for fire marshals and their teams to assemble in the main concourse in fifteen minutes.

FIVE

Time log: Day: 36,136. Hour: 12:52

"Why haven't you answered my calls, Noah? I must have left at least a dozen messages for you. I've found something!"

"Hello, Sage." Noah stopped, midstride, and loomed over her, a muscle jumping in his jaw. "How are you? I'm fine, by the way. Thanks for asking." He glared at her, letting his uncharacteristic rudeness sink in. "In case you hadn't noticed, I'm a little busy right now. We'll talk later." He stalked off.

For someone as mild-mannered as Noah to be both tense and rude, something big had to be up. Sage tried to keep up with his fast pace across the concourse and almost collided with one of the fire marshals.

A quick apology later, she'd caught up to him again and said, "Look, I know something's going on. Something about you is different, not to mention, I got a message to assemble with my fire team. That's never good." She grabbed him by the arm when it looked like she might lose him in the gathering crowd. "Noah, have you looked at my pictures? I really need you to look at them. Please?"

He glared at her again, then took a deep breath and wiped his face.

"What's happened?" she asked when she noticed the dried sweat and grime on his shirt.

"Firstly—no. I have been working, so I haven't looked at your pictures. Secondly, we'll explain in a minute, but trust me when I say, we are not in any danger." He turned to leave.

"Wait. You explain it to me now, Noah. The way you look makes me think you know more than you're letting on. And then there are the things I saw last night . . ." Her loud voice caught the attention of people nearby.

Noah groaned. "Fine. Jeez. Just keep your voice down." He ran a hand through his hair. "The manual fire sweep is because we don't fully trust the ship's sensor readings right now. We need to rule out fire as the cause of the rising heat and the ventilation malfunction. Now, please listen to your group leader's instructions."

Noah seemed more serious than usual. *No, not serious. Stressed.*

He went to speak to the head fire marshals. Ten minutes later, the marshals finished explaining the plan to their groups. Each group left the concourse headed to their designated inspection zones.

Sage hung back and scanned the concourse for Noah. When she spotted him, she quickly caught up. "I'm going with you. Did you forget I still have something I need to talk to you about?"

"Argh—this is seriously not a good time!"

"Just listen, please." She pleaded with her eyes.

Noah scowled but relented. "Fine, Sage. But make it quick."

She dived in. "I have a theory about what's happening. I need to show you the pictures I took last night." He shot her a sideways glance and she added, "I went for a walk. I couldn't sleep."

She pulled out her device and opened the photo gallery. The pictures stopped him in his tracks.

"Where did you take these?"

"Down near the pool."

"So, in the residential area?"

"Yes."

"And these?"

"The tennis courts."

"Jesus."

Noah never cursed and he ignored the bot that swept up to him with his paper fine. Sage reached for the slip. His eyes were glued to the images. For someone who wasn't quite twenty-five yet, he suddenly looked older than his years.

"What is it, Noah? It looks like rock or shell to me. A bit like mother-of-pearl." Sage was a natural sciences enthusiast. Had she grown up on Earth, she would probably have been a geologist or a marine biologist.

"Mother-of-pearl?"

"It's the coating on the inside of a seashell. Hard to explain unless you've seen it, but the mother-of-pearl makes the inside smooth for whatever lives in the shell. The pearlescence of this stuff" —she pointed at a photo— "reminds me of it. It's hard and smooth, almost silky."

"You touched it?"

Noah's exclamation made her jump.

"Sorry. I didn't know I shouldn't."

"Jesus!"

"Noah, I'm sorry. And I'm all right. What's the fuss?"

"We don't know what it is, that's what."

"So, you've also seen it?" She was elated. Usually, no one believed her when she came across something unusual.

"Well, not this specific form of it, but one whole

corner of the roof of a hangar in Section Two is covered in rock, and there's those stalactite things—"

"What? Are you serious?"

"Well, I think that's what they are. It's unreal. The columns looked like stalactites—at least from what I remember of our lessons on geology."

"That's incredible!"

"Hey! Are you two going to help with the fire inspection or just keep gabbing so the rest of us can't hear ourselves think?" The fire marshal glared at them. Their animated conversation had drawn the attention of the people around them.

"Sorry," Noah said, raising a hand, looking suitably chastised. He ushered Sage down a deserted corridor. When they were out of earshot of the angry fire marshal, he let her go. He leaned against the bulkhead and closed his eyes for a moment.

"Okay," he said, scrubbing at his face. "Let's think about this."

Sage waited patiently while he paced. She needed him on her side and this meant giving him space to get his head around what they might be dealing with.

A minute later he asked, "Can you tell me anything else from when you touched the rock?"

"I'm not sure what else I can say. It was smooth,

shiny and warm."

"Warm?"

"Yes. It was warm to the touch. Like it was being heated from the inside."

"Shit."

"You'd better stop doing that, or you're going to land up in the brig." She had never heard him swear in her whole life and now he'd done it three times in the last half hour. *He must be seriously worried.*

"Come on."

He took her arm again and they headed to Engineering.

"You do know you don't have to drag me behind you, right? I can walk on my own."

"Sorry." He let her go, looking awkward. "I'm just in a hurry. Try to keep up."

There was something about Noah's heightened anxiety and lapse of manners that she hardly wanted to acknowledge.

His behavior terrified her. His anxiety became her anxiety.

They were almost across the concourse when someone called after him.

It was Trigg. "Can we skip lunch? I'm not feeling great."

Sage gasped, surprised at how terrible the senior engineer looked. Trigg was pale and her expression was strained. Her face was swollen and puffy and sweat poured off her.

Noah didn't seem to notice. "That's okay. We have a minor emergency I'm trying to get on top of anyway."

Trigg scowled at Sage. It was no secret Noah's partner disliked her. She'd called Sage out a few times about the way she treated him. During their last confrontation, Trigg had told her to smarten up. Sage had told Trigg to mind her own business. Noah had broken up the beginnings of a physical scuffle between them. She still remembered the smirk on his face as he held them each at arm's length.

"Right. Go deal with your emergency then," Trigg said. "I can barely move my arm, so I'm going to get a stronger pain patch and sleep off this ache."

Sage yanked Noah's arm to get him to stop and talk to his partner. He gasped when Trigg's condition finally registered with him.

Her whole arm, bruised purple and swollen, hung limply at her side. Sage couldn't control her disgust. "Your arm looks awful."

"Wow! Thank you, Princess. I got hit by a space rock. I bet you think you'd look like a million bucks after that shit. Who even fucking asked you?"

Noah stepped in. "Trigg, Sage is right. Your arm doesn't look good. *You* don't look good. I think you need more than just pain meds. I think you need to get that injury looked at again."

"Fine. I'll get someone to check it out." She shot Sage a black look as she turned to leave.

Trigg shuffled in the direction of the infirmary. Noah and Sage exchanged a worried glance and continued through the crowded concourse towards Engineering.

The hairs on Sage's neck rose when, moments later, a piercing scream split the air and made everyone stop to find the source.

Trigg, down on all fours, with her left arm crooked and bent at a sickening angle, howled again. The injured limb appeared to break in several places and Sage gaped in horror when it snapped and twisted again.

"Oh, my God!" Noah raced to Trigg whose face had turned as white as the tiles at his feet. Her eyes were saucers of agony, and her skin was stretched unnaturally tight over her swollen features. A wave of nausea assaulted Sage. Trigg arched in pain, and her helpless cries became a panicked wheeze.

"Trigg? What's happening?" Noah looked around,

distraught and confused, and said, "Someone get a medic!"

He had reached out for Trigg's uninjured hand before Sage pulled him back. Bristling protrusions erupted from her torso and savaged her flesh. Bloody globs of skin and tissue sprayed, staining the white floor red.

"Trigg!" Noah's voice was hoarse with panic.

"Oh, God! Come away." Sage held onto him, standing between him and the grisly scene. In her terror, she kept her gaze averted, but a weak gurgle caused her to glance back.

Trigg's eyes rolled in her head and a ragged breath rushed from her mouth. The cracking of bones and snap of sinew overlayed the stunned silence in the concourse. All along Trigg's spine, thorny spikes tore through her skin. Her blood flowed and pooled. Someone sobbed, otherwise, everyone stood frozen.

Trigg's metamorphosis slowed. When crystals grew from her eyes and nose, Sage prayed the engineer was already dead. A shape defined by jagged crystal formations the color of bleached bone and gleaming red marbles obliterated everything that defined Trigg as she disappeared into the violent blooming.

Sage lunged for a large tree planter, barely making

it there before her stomach convulsed. Tears streamed down her face. She sobbed, weak and in shock.

Rapid footfalls at the far end of the concourse signaled the arrival of the medics.

Too late, thought Sage. *Too fucking late.*

What could they really have done for Trigg anyway? Sage wiped her mouth and looked over to where Noah knelt, weeping at the monstrous mass of rock and spikes. A shallow lake of sticky blood edged towards him.

He was in the path of the spilled blood, and it would soon reach him. Something about it touching him galvanized her and Sage raced to his side.

She gently tugged at his arm. "Come on, Noah. Get up." He ignored her. "Move!"

Noah shook his head, refusing to leave his friend. Sage's heart ached for him, the painful beats taking her breath away.

The medics ground to a halt nearby and gasped.

She dared a glance at the mass, which rested in a lumpy, red soup. Trigg had been eviscerated. In her place was a huge crystalline structure with menacingly sharp edges. It looked heavy and immovable, anchored to the floor it had stained with its arrival. An almost translucent crown of superfine titanium-white shards topped a forest of jagged red knives which grew out of bulging marbles of powdery maroon.

Sage swallowed and yanked at Noah again. The blood had almost reached his knees.

"You have to get back, Noah." She hauled against the big man with all her might and he finally moved a little. He looked up, not really seeing her, whimpered and slowly disconnected from the terrible scene.

He rose only to sag against her. Together, they staggered away from the deadly crystal mass and Sage wondered if she'd ever be able to forget what had just happened.

SIX

Time log: Day: 36,136. Hour: 14:04

"What the hell happened here?" The captain stood at the edge of the containment area. A group of robotic custodians were making slow work of the red smears around the mass. Captain Ellis grimaced and looked away.

"Lieutenant, make sure no one breaches the containment, unless it's Doctor Mills doing her examination and biohazard assessment."

"Yes, Captain." The lieutenant shifted and held up a bundle of blue fines in his hand. "Sir, what do you want me to do with these?"

The captain glanced at him. "Get rid of them. The ship etiquette program is suspended until this crisis is over."

"Yes, sir. How do we suspend the ship's etiquette program, sir?"

"Turn off the fucking AI, Lieutenant. That's how."

Sage watched the captain stalk away from the large

crowd of onlookers. She finished pouring a large coffee for Noah. They had retreated to the coffee shop after she had managed to get him away from the mass. By then medics and security personnel swarmed the area. The scene was quickly contained and Security began to question the bystanders. Captain Ellis arrived soon after she'd deposited a shaky and shocked Noah at a table. The captain's booming voice had hushed the crowd near the containment zone and he'd instructed them to go about their business as usual. He stayed only long enough to get a status report, issuing a stream of expletives as the story was recounted.

Sage liked the captain. He was competent and calm, but also realistic. He should be willing to listen to her theories, which she'd been mulling over for the last twenty minutes. Noah hadn't said a word since she'd dragged him away.

"Here. Drink this, Noah." She placed the coffee in front of her friend, smiling sympathetically. No one should see what they had witnessed today. The horror of it lingered.

After several minutes of silence, he finally picked up his cup and sipped the dark brew.

"Thanks, Sage." His voice was weak. "For everything. I'm sorry I was rude to you earlier." His sincerity unnerved her. He'd barely even looked at her in all the time she'd known him, and now it felt as if his eyes were boring into her soul.

"No problem. Least I could do," she mumbled then looked away, uncomfortable.

"Tell me." Her eyes flew back to his haggard features.

"What?"

"Tell me what you're thinking." He took another sip of coffee. "I see you looking over there, at that . . . thing. You've got some theory spinning around in your head, don't you?"

Sage sipped her drink and thought about the best way to state her suspicions. She didn't get many opportunities to tell someone her take on things. She took a deep breath and plunged in.

"Well, I think it's a life form."

Noah choked on his coffee. His eyes flew to hers. "What?"

"I think it's some kind of organic carbonate entity. It propagates like a life form does, and it's adapting like a life form would."

Noah glanced over his shoulder, frowning at the mass of heavy-looking crystal.

"But it looks like rock. How can rocks be living

things?"

"Have you ever heard of coral reefs?"

"Yes."

"Well, stony corals form a protective exoskeleton around their soft insides. That calcium-carbonate structure is called Aragonite, to be specific. Coral reproduces, adapts and grows. I believe that this," she directed her gaze at the mass, "is a type of Aragonite. It bears all the characteristics of it, from its color to its crystal structure, to its iridescence."

"You're saying this thing is a type of coral?"

"Well, I wouldn't go so far as to call it coral, but it's similar."

"Do you think it came from the asteroid strike?"

She nodded. "It's possible it was attached to the asteroid in a dormant state. Contact with our ship has somehow activated it."

"Sweet Jesus," Noah whispered. He shook his head slowly.

"Problem is, it appears to be parasitoid." Sage leaned forward and, with her expression a mix of sympathy and fear, she whispered, "And a parasitoid organism always kills its host. I think this thing may consume all of the organic matter on this ship if we don't stop it."

That was too far for Noah. He sat back in his chair, his skepticism plain to see.

"That's reaching, Sage, even for you."

"Thanks for the vote of confidence." She stood. His rejection of her theory hurt her deeply. Noah was the one person she'd trusted to believe her. He proved he was just like Ash and all the others who scoffed at her bold thinking. "Enjoy your coffee, Noah."

"Sage." She heard the chair skid back as he rose to follow her. "Sorry. That was too far."

"No. It was just far enough, Noah. As usual, I'm the conspiracy theorist with another crackpot theory. Don't come crying to me when one of those things rips you to shreds." She lashed out at his skepticism, but instantly regretted her words when he winced.

Noah put his mug in the receptacle at the door, and stalked out of the coffee shop without even a backward glance.

"God, Sage, what the hell was that?" she mumbled as he strode out of sight.

She trudged towards the lab, deep in thought. It was time to return to her normal duties, but she had little desire to do so. Soil analysis seemed unimportant in light of recent developments.

Sage didn't see an ensign running in her direction,

his attention on his device. The two collided and he exclaimed, "God! Sorry about that."

"Hey, what's the rush?" She rounded on him. He had almost knocked her down in his haste.

"There's a problem with the elevators. I'm trying to get to the bridge, but it appears to be cut off. I have to take the emergency access shaft," he said impatiently.

"Is the command crew on the bridge? Are they aware of the situation?"

"I believe so. They're trying to find a way to open the access stairs, but the doors are also jammed."

If the command crew got cut off from the rest of the ship, the *Vega Four* would be in serious trouble. "Shit." Panic blossoming, she fell into step beside the hurrying ensign.

"Your language, ma'am," he said automatically.

The two of them stared at each other for a moment. Nothing happened. No bots swooped in waving blue slips.

"That's new. No demerits."

"Yeah." The ensign blinked and shrugged. When he noticed Sage was still with him, he shot her a curious look.

"I'm coming with you. Knowing what I know, I think it's best if we move in groups," she said.

The young man didn't argue but looked unsettled.

They located the access panel for the vast escape shaft system that ran through the whole ship. They climbed in and crept along a low, narrow tube. At an intersection of multiple tunnels, a set of ladders led to different decks above and below.

Sage followed the ensign up one of the ladders, heading for the bridge access shaft. They climbed for what seemed like forever, the ladder disappearing into the darkness of the tube above them. Slightly breathless, Sage swallowed hard. She tried to ignore the burning ache in her tired muscles as she climbed and climbed. The heat and humidity in the tube were suffocating and it was with great relief that they finally stepped off the ladder and onto a narrow platform. Another tunnel led them out of the shaft into a circular forecourt at the entrance to the bridge.

"I love how spacious the tubes up here are." The ensign grinned.

"Well, we can't expect the commanders of our ship to be crawling around on their hands and knees in the case of an emergency, now can we?" She imagined that the captain's cabin had room enough to host a sit-down gathering if desired. Even though she didn't believe in the system, she muttered, "Class privilege exists wherever there are people. It maintains the hierarchy and order of things."

The ensign didn't comment. He straightened his uniform and Sage smoothed her hair. It normally frizzed in the shower and the humidity in the tubes had given her a copper halo she couldn't tame.

"Never mind your hair. I'm sure you won't be in there long enough for anyone to notice. The captain won't be at all pleased to have a civilian on his bridge."

"Thanks for the vote of confidence, um—jeez! I didn't ask you your name." Embarrassed by the oversight, she added beet red ears to her already disheveled appearance.

"Ensign Tay Fine, ma'am. And you are?"

"Hi, Tay. I'm Sage Lang."

"Well, Sage, are we ready?" The ensign straightened and assumed a stiff, military demeanor.

"I hope so," she said, a knot tightening in her midsection. If Noah wouldn't listen, perhaps the captain might. What did she have to lose by trying?

They stood in front of the doors and the ensign touched the control panel. The doors glided silently open and Sage gasped.

The roomy bridge was a hive of activity, full of screen arrays and glowing workstations. A large screen filled the center of the back wall and showed a variety of data about the voyage and ship systems. When it refreshed, the data was replaced by a massive expanse of black, broken only by the twinkle of distant stars. Sage's mouth sagged. It was the first time she'd seen live feed of what was beyond the ship.

"Ensign Fine, did you bring a guest to the bridge?" A terse question directed at the now ramrod straight ensign next to Sage made her scalp prickle.

"Apologies for the intrusion, Lieutenant Commander," Sage said to the hostile looking officer, "but I have something important to tell the captain regarding the formation in the concourse."

"Did I address you, ma'am?" He levelled a withering look at her and Sage lost the ability to speak. Ensign Fine stepped in to rescue her from the commander's intimidating stare.

"Lieutenant Commander Gray, this is Sage Lang. She told me she has information pertinent to the situation in the concourse that is of a sensitive nature and should be directed to the captain at his earliest convenience, sir." Tay had not moved a muscle apart from those he needed to bark a response. The commander barred their access to the bridge until he was satisfied their business was important enough to warrant their presence.

"I know who Miss Lang is, Ensign. We dated briefly in high school." His eyes raked her from bottom to top.

"Sir?"

Sage almost smiled when she finally recognized Dylan Gray. She hadn't seen much of him since high school. He had gone on to do training at the crew academy and probably spent the majority of his time working and socializing in those circles.

His hair was short and his cap obscured his serious features. A neat beard completed his disguise. She hadn't instantly recognized him because the man before her was a far cry from the boy she had known.

His expression softened. The moment he caught Sage's gaze, he gave her a conspiratorial wink. The quick exchange suggested the brassiness of his manner was routine. Gray was required to defend the sanctity of the bridge.

But she had good reason to be there. Ensign Fine had given a compelling argument for her presence.

"Ensign, Miss Lang, follow me, please." Gray led them around the gallery and down a gangway to a door. The door slid open and they entered a small conference room. A table with six chairs and a neat bookcase full of ancient volumes greeted them.

"I will speak to the captain. Wait here."

When he left, the ensign relaxed for a moment and fiddled with his device, preparing the data he had come to deliver to Captain Ellis.

"Thanks for the explanation back there. Glad one of us was prepared for that greeting."

"You're welcome. I do this enough to know how to handle the Lieutenant Commander. He's tough, but fair."

Noted, thought Sage. *He's also not bad looking.*

The door slid open and Ensign Fine snapped to attention again and saluted. Sage stood a little straighter, feeling awkward and out of place around the rigor of non-civilian etiquette. Her courage threatened to desert her. She prayed the ensign's business with Captain Ellis would be brief. It would be deeply embarrassing if she couldn't articulate her thoughts on the Aragonite mass that had consumed Trigg.

The men shared a clipped exchange and Ensign Fine took his leave, with a quick look over his shoulder at Sage. She registered pity and relief in the ensign's expression as the door closed after him.

Traitor, she thought with mild amusement. *Throw me to the wolves and then run away.*

"Miss Lang." Captain Ellis's voice boomed in the

small room. "Take a seat."

Sage obediently pulled out a chair and sat down.

The captain followed suit and the door slid open to admit the chief commander and Lieutenant Commander Gray. They both sat down at the table and she swallowed hard, suddenly finding the conference room stuffy.

"Gray, please pour Miss Lang a glass of water. She looks thirsty," Captain Ellis instructed in a milder tone. He sat back in his chair, swinging an ankle up over one knee.

He waited for her to have a sip of water then asked, "What is it you know about the rock mass that killed my engineer?"

"Sir, I believe it's a bio-composite, an organic life form similar to stony coral. We have three formations that have already been observed: crystalline, smooth bulbous, and stalactite."

"Really?" He glared at Sage. "A lifeform?"

"How do you think it got inside the ship?" The question came from Dylan Gray.

"The asteroid strike left debris floating around the ship. Trigg—sorry, First Engineer Larsson—was struck by some of the debris and it embedded itself in her arm." Sage shrugged, still trying to piece it together.

"But we do a bio-sweep and deep decontamination

on anyone who does EVA." The captain appeared thoughtful. He was listening, measuring her words.

Sage grew bolder. "Sir, the object that struck her penetrated, then burrowed and finally, attached itself to the bone of her arm before the sweep and decon." Noah had filled her in earlier on Trigg's accident and subsequent visit to the infirmary. Her assumption was the fragment had been quick to secure itself to its host.

"There's no way to know for sure if that's true, but it would be one of the only ways for something to survive decon, sir." The chief commander said. "It would have had to attach to Trigg's arm in order to pass the bio-sweep." His words made Sage feel better about her theory.

"Jesus Christ."

"Captain, the entity also penetrated the ship's ice shield somehow. There's evidence of it all over the ship. I suspect it found its way into the ventilation system, seeking the warmth and humidity it needed in there." She again reached beyond her understanding into the purely theoretical.

"What evidence have you seen? I understand from our engineering team that there's a mass in Section Two. What else is there?"

"In the recreation complex, there are areas that

have developed a combined crystalline and bulbous crust on the walls, ceiling and floors. It looked to me as if it spread via the ventilation ducts, and so it's logical to assume that's also how the contamination happened in Section Two."

The men were glancing at each other with earnest concern.

"I'll need to speak to your supervisor. Lieutenant Quinn will need to confirm all of this," said Captain Ellis. Sage knew in that moment that the captain was familiar with her reputation for dramatics. "I'm sure it's probably nothing more than harmless calcium deposits caused by the offline ventilation system. Engineering are working, as we speak, to get those systems back up and running." He rose from the table, signaling the end of the meeting.

"You don't believe me?" Sage couldn't hide her disappointment.

"No, I believe that you saw deposits, but I think it's a stretch to think that what you saw is alive." The captain smiled down at her, an indulgent look on his face. He was ready to dismiss her and Sage lunged for her last chance to be heard. Standing quickly, she smacked her hand down on the table.

"That thing *is* alive! And we need to stop it before

more people die. This whole ship is full of organic material it can consume. It's not going to stop until it runs out of an energy source." She breathed hard, her nostrils flaring. The force of her conviction made her heart race. "*We* are the energy source—our blood, our flesh—we're full of warm, salty fluids, and proteins."

Gray parried. "Sage, come on, be serious for a minute. There is zero evidence to suggest we're dealing with an alien life form that's invaded our ship." He glanced at the captain who had stiffened at her abrasive defiance. "I mean, what are the odds of something like that happening out here?"

"Thank you for your input, Miss Lang. Gray, please show our guest off my bridge. I have actual work to do." Captain Ellis stalked out of the conference room.

"Shit."

"Come on, Sage. It's his job to be objective. It's not personal." That was a lie, and they both knew it, but the commander was trying to soften the blow and she appreciated the effort.

He escorted her back up to the gallery and stood with her a moment more at the exit.

"Dylan, please, I'm begging you. You have to believe me." He was her last chance to do something about the invasive mass.

He smiled at the use of his first name and sighed. "I tell you what, I'm off duty in an hour. Come find me at the Pizza Palace. Tell me everything you know and show me some evidence."

Sage beamed, thrilled that he was at least willing to give her another chance to explain. "I'll see what I can dig up between now and then."

"Hey," he called after her. The bridge doors slid open. "Don't you have a job you're supposed to be at right now?"

"This is more important." Sage sensed the dramatic events of the day would be swept away quietly if she didn't fully investigate what was happening to the ship and its occupants. She knew she'd be in trouble with her supervisor, but she had a mission, and the ship's survival depended on it. "I'm doing this for everyone. My family. Yours. Everyone's in danger if we don't act now. I'll beg time off. I have real work to do." An idea formed and she smiled at the young commander. "See you in an hour, Dylan."

SEVEN

Time log: Day: 36,136. Hour: 16:33

Sage dropped the big bag of equipment and protective clothing next to the door to the pool facility. She pulled out a hazmat suit, slid her feet out of her resin boots and donned the heavy silicon overall and hood. She squeezed her feet back into the squeaky footwear after tugging the bulky suit up to her hips. Sage blew a strand of hair out of her face, panting at the effort it took to get the suit on unassisted.

God, this thing is heavy and huge!

It was against the rules to take a hazmat suit out of the lab without a work order, but she knew that no one else would help her. She'd burned too many bridges with her colleagues to ask them for a favor.

Sealing herself inside, she tried to ignore how hot she was already. The suit's stuffiness caused spells of nausea and she knew that if she wasn't quick, she risked fainting from heat exhaustion.

The doors for the pool deck barely opened wide

enough for her to squeeze through. After dragging the bag in behind her, she turned to survey the gloomy room. The walls were shimmering. The entire pool facility glowed with iridescent mother-of-pearl crust. The only exception was the deck directly around the pool and the pool itself. The atmospheric changes and heat had turned the water into an algae-green sludge.

Sage gulped. She stepped gingerly towards the edge of the pool deck, eyeing the crystal growth with a mix of apprehension and wonder. Holding her device steady, she pressed Record and panned around the room. The video was the first bit of evidence Sage needed. It would help corroborate her findings. When she thought she had enough footage, the device was securely stowed in the bag.

Okay, Sage. Get the samples and get out. Sweat ran down her back and strands of damp hair clung to her forehead. Her pulse raced. The creepy, other-worldliness of the transformed space unsettled her.

She grabbed a scraper, chisel, hammer, tongs, and jars from the bag, putting everything into her tool belt. She picked up the biohazard cooler she would stow the samples in, checking how cool it was. The cooler's temperature would need to be reset to resemble the conditions of the pool complex if she hoped to return to the lab with viable samples.

When Sage was all set, she looked for the most mature deposits, finding them on the far wall, beyond the pool. The wall was darkly opalescent. The rainbow-colored layers gleamed invitingly. She picked her way around the pool and set the cooler down next to her.

With trembling hands, she held the scraper and a jar and took a shaky breath.

I have no idea what's going to happen when I harvest these samples, but I have to try. Everything rides on physical proof. This is not the time to chicken out.

She closed her eyes briefly then ever so carefully approached the wall. The scraper skidded over the smooth, hard surface and she pulled back, waiting to see if there would be any kind of response from the stony edifice. Her mind raced with images of the bloom that had ripped Trigg to shreds only a short time ago. She tapped the surface again and waited.

Nothing. Good. See, Sage? It's fine. Keep going. Just keep going.

She raised the scraper. This time she dug the point in and wiggled it to loosen a thin sliver of the rainbow crust. It dropped into the jar she held and Sage breathed a little easier, screwing the lid over the sample.

Next, she tried a different spot closer to the

ventilation duct where the deposits were more irregular. The lumpy, scaly mounds reminded Sage of calcium deposits from hard water experiments she'd conducted in the lab.

She tried to scrape some loose, but the tool skidded over the unyielding surface with little effect.

"Damn."

She switched to a chisel and a small hammer. Before she struck the chisel, she glanced around to check her status, sensing she was being observed. The room appeared deserted, the entity unchanged, and she returned to her task, ignoring the gooseflesh that crept up her damp back.

"Okay, just a small piece, Sage, and then you're done." The heat made her clothes and the hazmat suit clammy. It was suffocating and she couldn't wait to be out of this place and the irritating suit.

She rested the tip of the chisel against a lumpy growth and tapped the back of the tool with her hammer. She heard a faint crack and tapped the chisel again.

A small shard broke off and dropped to the deck. She bent to pick it up with her tongs. When she straightened, sharp spikes had sprung from the notch her chisel had made. The spikes grew at such a rapid pace, she could see it happening. Mesmerized, she gave a low whistle, forgetting her fear for a moment as her scientist-self marveled at the shimmering crystals.

Something touched the back of her suit leg. It brought her sharply out of her reverie and she swiveled, her senses on high alert. Sage faced a bristling wall of growing crystal daggers. They were all pointed at her.

"Jesus!" She jumped and, without thinking, brought her hammer down on the one touching her suit, yelping as she did so. She smashed her way through the bristling spikes to where she'd left her bag, gasping for air as she fought her revulsion and terror. The inside of the hood's visor fogged. Her breathing was fast and erratic, causing suit alarms to sound. She tried not to panic. In her haste, she'd forgotten to secure the sample cooler's strap to the slippery suit and the box slipped from her shoulder. It tumbled, coming to rest at the edge of the green pool.

"Oh, God!"

She adjusted the hood to see better and grabbed for the cooler, all the while glancing left and right, horrified by the pursuing crystal growths. With no time to lose, she scooped up the rest of her gear and peered through the fogged visor, searching for the safest route back to the doors.

The spikes rapidly sprung from all the smooth surfaces close to her, the entity's defenses clearly activated by her sample harvest. Some of the sharp growths were arm-length spears. It was impossible to stay calm and tears blurred her already misted view out the hood.

"God help me!" she wailed, her focus on survival and escape.

Fighting for air and at the verge of passing out, she ran through the bristling field towards the exit. The barbed spears pursued her, almost catching her a few times as she quickly side-stepped barbs that could impale her. Bizarrely, the spear-length growths seemed aware of her path, aggressively defending the main rocky edifice behind her. The surface area of the mass dwindled near the doors. The closer she got to the exit, the fewer spikes blossomed around her, but Sage wasn't taking any chances.

I'm getting the hell out of here!

Still wearing the hazmat suit, she squeezed back through the narrow opening between the doors. The bag snagged and she groaned, weeping at the unexpected delay. It was wedged sideways in the opening. She yanked at it until it pulled free and she fell back, the bag landing next to her. Sage scrambled to her feet, lunged for the access panel and slammed a gloved hand on the close button. She initiated a lockdown of the area and the door bolts slid home.

Gasping, retching and in tears, Sage ignored decontamination protocols and clawed at her hood. She threw it off then pushed and yanked at the suit to free herself of it. She sucked in large gulps of air, finally rid of the cloying heat. Still panicked, she checked her legs for scratches. None of the crystal protrusions that touched the suit seemed to have pierced it, at least. Her relief was short lived. The shock of her terrifying flight soon overwhelmed her. Bathed in sweat, she sank to the floor, her legs unable to hold her up anymore. She sat in her tank top and shorts and sobbed.

It took a few moments for her to calm down and when she did, she regarded the cooler with heavy dread. The benign-looking samples rested inside. She knew better.

This thing has an aggressive defense mechanism which it deploys with lethal speed. There's no way it's just a bit of fucking rock!

When her head stopped spinning and she could better control the urge to throw up, she got to her feet and gathered her things. She walked on shaky legs to the lab and deposited everything on the floor near her workstation.

The lab was quiet. When she'd been there earlier to collect the equipment for the sample harvest, everyone had been leaving to attend the end-of-cycle meeting in the greenhouse complex. She'd managed to avoid her supervisor, and her colleagues had left her alone. No one seemed to notice that she didn't follow the group to the meeting.

Sage got to work and set the collected samples out on the bench by her microscope. There was a lot to do and not much time to do it in. It took a while for her hands to stop shaking and she fought the urge a few times to just burst into tears.

"Come on, Sage. This is important. Get it together and get the samples analyzed," she said, taking a series of steadying breaths. She leaned over the microscope and lost herself in her observations.

With some results logged, she checked the time on the wall clock. *Almost five.* She had a few minutes to get a change of clothes before meeting Dylan Gray.

"Well, at least I now have proof he'll be able to see for himself and then we can show the captain."

In her cabin, Sage changed into a fresh shirt and pants and went to the concourse.

She was exhausted now that the adrenalin of her

terror-filled escape from the pool facility had worn off, but she reminded herself there was no time to rest. As if to drive the point home, she caught sight of small bulges of bone-colored deposits rimming the corridor ventilation ducts. She shuddered and suppressed her burgeoning dread. She had an awful sense that the *Vega Four* was under serious threat.

All around her, life carried on as normal. No one else noticed the peculiar growths or the increasingly stifling confines of the ship. Was she imagining the crew's lack of urgency, or was it that her recent encounters with the invasive entity had given her a horrifying perspective of what they were really up against?

EIGHT

Time log: Day: 36,136. Hour: 17:20

"Noah?" Sage hesitated to speak to him because of the way they had left things earlier.

"I'm busy," came the clipped reply. "These ventilation controls won't fix themselves."

"I know. It's just—"

He spun around, to find Sage and Dylan Gray standing together. They both wore the same tight expression and they both looked scared.

This brought him up short. Noah had never seen Dylan be anything other than cocky and over-confident. The strained look on the commander's face was sobering.

"Okay. What has the two of you so freaked out?"

"Take a look at this." Sage handed him her device with a recording ready to go. He hit Play and watched the video of her first observations in the pool complex, and another recording of a microscope slide.

While he watched, Dylan filled him in. "Sage told

me she had an encounter with the crystalline entity in the rec complex when she went down to the pool to gather samples," Dylan said. "She came to me and explained what she'd seen and that she had samples in the Science lab. Back in the lab, we put a few slivers under the microscope. Then we prodded them with a needle to try to replicate the behavior she experienced."

"Why would you do that?"

"Keep watching the microscope video. You'll see," Sage said.

"Whoa!" Noah gaped at the screen. "Did that thing just grow spikes?"

"Yep."

"And they follow the needle. That's . . . that's . . ."

"Incredibly disturbing," Dylan finished. Noah shook his head in disbelief.

"Shit! That's not good. And this happened when you collected your samples?" He looked at Sage, his eyes wide.

"A whole section of this thing came after me. I barely got out of there." Sage took the device back from him and blinked. Her eyes were bright with unshed tears. She fairly vibrated with distress.

"Sage, I'm sorry. That must have been harrowing. Especially after—"

"Yes. It was. No need to remind me, thanks."

"We need to get this in front of Captain Ellis," Noah said.

"I tried to talk to the captain earlier after we argued." Her glance flitted to Dylan then back again. "He dismissed my concerns, and I know that's my fault for being a pain in his ass."

"But that was before you had proof," Dylan said. "He'll listen to you now. I'm sure of it."

"He's right. That recording is incredible. It's undeniable proof we're in imminent danger. I'm sorry I didn't listen to you earlier." Noah packed up his tools. Tackling ventilation system repairs no longer seemed like his top priority.

"That's okay. All forgotten." Sage paused and hugged her device against her chest. "Guys, we might need more than a video of crystal growth on a microscope slide," she said. "I mean, this doesn't really convey the danger. The captain's not likely to have left the bridge since he was down in the concourse earlier, and even after seeing that thing for himself, he dismissed my theories. It's possible he still has only a limited grasp of the potential threat we're facing."

"True," Dylan said. "The captain made repairs our top focus. I don't know if he's even ordered Lieutenant

Quinn to investigate the rock formations yet."

"So, he might dismiss this on the grounds that it's come from Sage and not her boss?" Noah's expression darkened when Dylan shrugged his confirmation. The captain would need hard evidence to take swift action. "Then we'll have to record an attack like the one you experienced when you harvested your samples."

"Christ, that's taking a helluva risk! Is that our only option?" Dylan looked upset.

"I think so. We need the evidence to be irrefutable."

"Noah's right. Come on." Sage tucked the device in her pocket and left Engineering with the two men in tow. They marched through the ship, heading back to the pool.

"Are we going back inside?" Noah asked, not liking that idea at all.

"Yeah. If we can get the doors open."

When they approached the locked doors of the pool facility, she put up a hand and stopped them well short of the control panel. The trio stood awestruck. A huge mass of shimmering, crystalline crust had sprouted from the sliver of gap between the shut doors and emerged through the access control panel.

"There's no way we're getting in there now," Dylan said, frowning.

"No, but there may be enough of the mass out here to produce the reaction we're looking for." Sage stepped forward and Noah reached out to stop her.

"I don't like this. You've taken enough chances today already. Let me do it."

Sage glanced at Dylan and he nodded. Noah, relieved to see the commander agreed with him, also caught something else in the look Dylan gave Sage. The sour taste of jealousy caught him by surprise. But now was not the time. He focused his anger on the reason they were there.

"Damn. I should've brought a hammer or drill. See if you can find something I can use to hit this thing with." The three scattered.

"Anything?" he asked Sage when she came back down the corridor.

"No. And I see you're empty-handed too."

"Here." Dylan returned and handed him a length of pipe.

"Where did you get that?"

"Don't ask."

Sage grinned.

Noah thought, *we're all breaking the rules today.*

"Okay. I guess, just try to tap it first." She stepped back and balled her fists.

"That's not helping, Sage." Her obvious anxiety was contagious. Noah felt himself tensing up. "If you can't watch, then look away."

Dylan chuckled. "Come on, just hit the thing, already. I'll record you."

"Jesus. Fine." Noah gulped. Apprehension shivered up his spine. He cautiously approached the control panel, looking for a weak point to strike. The balls of rock crystal were covered with spikes as long as his hand.

He lifted the pipe, glanced at the other two and hesitated, almost losing his nerve. Sage had covered her eyes and was leaning away. Dylan's steady gaze held a challenge and Noah's resolve stiffened.

He swung the metal bar down and struck a clanging blow against the spiked mass.

"Nothing happened," Dylan said, his voice sounding muffled through the ringing in Noah's ears.

"I can see *that*," he said.

"You need to hit it harder. If you can't, maybe step aside and let me try."

Dylan's tone mocked him, and the experiment became a duel—who would chicken out first?

"Shut up and do the damned recording. And move back. You're too close, Dylan."

"Hit it harder this time." Sage had lost some of her fear and was standing closer.

He nodded, lifted the pipe over his shoulder like a baseball bat, and threw his weight behind his next strike.

The blow shattered the crystal mass. A cloud of glassy shards rained over Noah's arms and shoulders. He yelped and shook particles off his shirt and hands. Revulsion threatened to overwhelm him. He calmed himself, then saw Sage's curious trepidation transform into shock.

"Noah, look out!"

Dylan yanked him to the ground as a massive spike erupted from the control panel and buried itself in the wall opposite.

"Shit!" Sage covered her eyes and ducked as more shards flew.

"Thanks for pulling me away." Noah stared, pale and wide-eyed, at the jagged spear of crystal emerging from the control panel. "That thing would have skewered me."

It was hard to believe the speed and ferocity of the crystal's growth. It made a sound like static electricity and twisting metal. The high-pitched squeaking as it buried itself in the wall hurt Noah's ears.

"Did you record that?" His voice quavered. The shock would take a while to wear off.

"I got it. There's a bit of motion blur from when I grabbed you, but you can see the spike development and its trajectory. It was aiming straight at the middle of your chest."

In silence, they watched the playback. Noah had to look away. The deadly accuracy unnerved him.

"Come on," Sage said. "We have to show Captain Ellis."

"Not yet."

"What?" The other two said simultaneously, both staring at Dylan.

"I think we need to do at least one more demo. The captain is going to need more than this video. One is a coincidence. Two will get him to sit down and watch. Three will convince him."

"You mean we need to do that two more times?" Noah's voice rose.

"Noah," Sage paused and looked at the crystals, "you know Dylan's right. We need more evidence."

"Ah, crap." He sighed heavily. "Okay, but you need to move way back this time. It's had some warning and there's no telling what the next response will be."

Noah grabbed the pipe and walked towards the

crusted doors.

"Wait. I want to take a crack at it." Dylan held out a hand for the pipe. "Can't have you hogging all the fun jobs." Noah's glance slid from Dylan to Sage. She'd paled visibly.

"You sure you're up to it?" Noah asked.

"Just get me out of the way if that thing comes for me, all right?"

"Dylan." Sage went over to speak quietly to him and Noah walked away to lean on the wall down the corridor, out of earshot. He couldn't understand what she saw in the commander. He was an arrogant, self-obsessed glory hound.

Noah overheard him say to her, "It's okay. Now step back. Noah, we're ready."

He returned, ready to rush to the other man's aid. Sage stood halfway behind a bulkhead, her hands clutching the device.

Dylan swung the pipe up on his shoulder and stepped up to the spiked mass with cocky assurance. He smiled at them, and Noah resisted rolling his eyes.

"Recording."

"Ready?" Dylan winked at Sage.

Noah huffed. "Just get on with your demo and stop messing around."

With a big wind up, Dylan aimed for the middle of the spike that had launched itself at Noah earlier. But before he could get a strike in, the thick trunk of the spike bloomed with new growths. Long, sabre-length shards sprouted, all aimed at Dylan.

"Get back, it's going to shoot those things at you!" Noah yelled as a long spear erupted from the shape-changing mass.

Dylan hit the floor and scrambled towards them. The spear streaked down the corridor and smashed onto the floor twenty meters away.

"Good God!" Sage rushed to help him and they all scampered out of the way of more spikes that launched in their direction.

They retreated down the corridor, the crystal spears crashing behind them in shattering explosions.

"I think we can go to the captain with these videos. I don't think that thing is going to let us near it again," Noah said with a gasp.

"It defended itself preemptively. That demonstrates cognition." Sage looked from Dylan to Noah. "I don't quite believe it, but—"

"Sentience," Dylan said and shook his head slowly.

"We're in big trouble." Noah looked back down the corridor. The fallen spears had begun to bloom more spikes. The corridor leading to the pool facility was now impassable. He sensed a simmering anger but wondered if he wasn't just projecting his own feelings onto the rock entity. "Let's go."

NINE

Time log: Day: 36,136. Hour: 17:56

"Hurry!" Sage led the way through the tubes and back up the long ladder shaft to the bridge deck.

Noah scratched at an itchy spot on his neck. There was an uncomfortable prickle under his skin and it only took him a moment to reach a conclusion. His realization caused him to almost lose his footing on the ladder and Dylan yelled up at him from several rungs below in the dimly lit tunnel.

"Hey! Take it easy. If you fall, I fall."

"Sorry. My hands are sweaty. It's unbelievably hot in here." Noah tried to deflect but caught the tremor in his own voice.

It's only a matter of time before I have to tell the others I've been infected like Trigg.

Struggling with a wave of emotions, he worked to recover his balance and resume climbing.

Dylan was slow to respond, breathless when he said, "Well, I've already done this twice today, so I know what you mean."

"We're almost there," Sage said, her voice echoing.

A moment later, she stepped off the ladder onto the narrow platform. Noah and Dylan followed and, one by one, they exited the tube system. The air felt cooler and more breathable in the corridor.

"This way." Dylan walked ahead. He swiped his hand over the bridge access controls and the quick glide of the doors revealed alarming chaos beyond.

"Where's the captain?" Noah directed the question at an ensign furiously tapping at her control panel.

"Dunno. Ask Nav."

"Gray! Where have you been?" The bridge chief barked.

"Apologies, sir. I went to help with sampling of the crystalline structure. We have evidence we urgently need to show Captain Ellis." Dylan stood to attention, his Adam's apple bobbing.

"Captain Ellis is in a meeting with the Engineering chief. He can't be disturbed."

"Oh, I think the captain's going to want to speak to us," Sage said. "We have time-sensitive and critically important material to share on the entity that's taking over this ship."

The chief levelled a severe look on her. Noah stepped in to save her from a tongue-lashing she partially deserved for addressing the chief so insolently.

"Sir, we have reason to believe the ship is under attack." Noah plunged in. "We have proof."

"What?"

"Look."

Noah produced the device they'd recorded the entity on. The chief watched both recordings without so much as a flinch but the moment the last video concluded, he said, "Follow me."

The group strode along the gallery to the bridge conference room. The door slid open, and the heated discussion inside abruptly stopped.

"Chief, I said no interr—"

"My apologies, Captain. Both you and Bo need to see this." He handed the captain the device.

They watched the videos through. Bo whistled and his expression grew worried.

"What am I seeing here, exactly?" The captain looked up. Noah watched a hint of recognition flit across the man's face as his gaze rested on Sage's pale face.

"The crystalline entity is defending itself, sir." She paused and almost breathlessly added, "Preemptively. It appears to be aware that it's under attack."

"Impossible."

"Captain, we were all there," Dylan said. Noah hoped the lieutenant commander's corroboration would add the right amount of gravitas. He added his own nod to the argument.

"Not possible," repeated the captain. He stood and slid the device back across the table to Noah.

"Sir, that thing is going to overrun the whole ship within a matter of days, possibly less. We need to put the entire population on alert and lock down the exposed areas while we try and figure out—"

"I'm not putting the entire population on lockdown!" The captain's chest rose and fell, his hard stare settling on each of them for a moment. Then, sounding a little more composed, he asked, "Have you any idea of the panic an order like that would cause?"

"Sir, we—"

"No!" Captain Ellis's expression stopped any further argument.

Noah watched the pulse throb in the captain's neck. He swiveled to regard Sage, who looked crestfallen. He waited to be dismissed, angry and disappointed that the captain seemed so resistant to their pleas for action.

"You have to understand," Captain Ellis said, and Noah stopped and turned. "I can't cause a panic and leave everyone locked in their quarters, waiting for that *thing* to get them. Help is weeks, maybe months away. We'll all be dead if we wait for a rescue."

There was an air of defeat about the captain as he spoke. Noah's dread grew. His neck prickled again and he forced himself not to react. He clenched his fist against his thigh, fighting the urge to scratch at the crystal splinter burrowing under his skin.

"Get Chief Science Officer Quinn in here." The captain addressed his bridge chief who then left the room in search of Mara. "In the meantime, let's discuss what we can do to beat this thing."

Sage grinned at Noah. He tried to smile back. It was already too late for him, but he would die helping his friends survive.

They sat down at the table with the captain. Sometime later, the bridge chief returned.

"I was unable to locate Lieutenant Quinn, sir. I've left word at the lab for her to come to the bridge as soon as she can."

"Thank you, Chief."

The discussion went round the table, everyone making suggestions, but nothing close to a viable option came up until Sage finally said, "We need to figure out the entity's vulnerabilities."

"If it has any." Dylan flopped back in his chair,

frustrated.

"It must have vulnerabilities," Sage said. "Think about it—it was probably dormant in space, buried in the asteroid. No light, no heat, no atmosphere."

"Atmosphere—yes." Noah could see where she was leading them. "The ventilation shut down and the crystals created a warm, humid atmosphere in which to propagate. If we cut off the heat and the humidity, we starve it of two things it needs—water and warmth."

"But how do we do that with the whole ship?" The chief engineer shook his head. "The entire system offline is my worst nightmare. I mean, what if we can't get it back up and running?"

"Then we shut off sections at a time, starve it out, bit by bit."

"Sage has a point. But that thing is everywhere." Noah doubted they'd be able to stop it with a section-by-section shut down. "We'd have to make sure it has no escape routes from the cut off sections we trap it in."

"Here's what we need to do first." The captain stepped in and issued instructions. "We slow it down—cut off the heat, isolate a section of the ship and vent the humidity. In the meantime, we create safe zones. That might buy us the time we need to figure out what destroys that thing."

"Are the safety zones supposed to be areas the entity hasn't reached yet?"

"Exactly." Captain Ellis pursed his lips. "I hesitate to call it an entity, but we need to secure those zones and move everyone into them."

"Then we exterminate the rock-bastard." Bo sounded enthusiastic, and Noah smiled. He liked his chief. He would miss working with him.

"Extermination. Yes. If that's possible," said Captain Ellis.

"Let's go find out how to stop this thing," Sage said. Ignoring the astonished looks from the officers, she headed for the door.

"Miss Lang, you were not dismissed," said the bridge chief.

"Ah, jeez. Sorry, Captain." Sage's cheeks turned peach pink and she stopped.

Captain Ellis put her out of her misery. "Keep me posted on Sciences' progress, Miss Lang. Chief Nash," said the captain, his attention on the old engineer. "Get me your crew's solutions for the extermination. As fast as you can, please."

"Yes, sir!"

They left the conference room. Bo, Noah, and Sage

made their way over to the bridge exit.

"Be careful, Sage." Dylan looked at Noah. "Keep each other safe."

Noah didn't know what to say to that. The crystal shard burned under his skin, a grim reminder that his own fate was sealed.

TEN

Time log: Day: 36,136. Hour: 18:41

While Sage bent over her lab bench, Noah, her semi-reluctant baby-sitter, paced the room.

"You don't have to stay, you know."

"I think it's best if we stick together. For safety reasons and at least for as long as Bo doesn't need me."

"Well, I appreciate the company. With everything that's happened today, I'm not comfortable sitting here alone with the crystal samples." He gave her a reassuring nod and she got back to work.

An hour passed.

"Do you have anything?" he asked when she sat back and stretched.

"I might, but I'll need to prove it's going to be a definitive solution."

"What do you mean?"

"So, when I was on the pool deck earlier, I noticed the crystals didn't grow anywhere near the pool itself. There also wasn't any evidence of it in the water."

"But the entity needs moisture. Why didn't it overrun the pool?"

"My question, exactly." Sage nodded and showed him some readings. "This is the pH of the pool at last reading. And this is the measure of pH in the ventilation filters at last reading."

"The pool readings show the pH as mildly acidic. That pool is chlorinated."

"And the ventilation is just off neutral on the alkaline side."

"So, the entity avoided the acidic water because it's bad for it?"

"I think so. The entity's structure appears to be primarily calcium carbonate in crystal and solid mass form. Calcium carbonate is naturally alkaline. It dissolves in acids."

"Wait—I have to ask—if acids dissolve it, how was it possible for that thing to completely take over in Trigg's body?"

They both frowned. It felt like years had passed since that horrific incident in the concourse, but barely six hours had elapsed.

"You're wondering about stomach acid?" she asked. "There was probably not enough. At least that's my guess. Blood is mildly alkaline and there's way more of it in a human body. About five liters, give or take."

"So, it took over all of Trigg's other systems and avoided her stomach?"

"I don't want to even consider how it would have known to avoid her digestive system."

They stared at each other for a moment.

Noah looked back at the screen. "We're getting off track. So—the pool acid thing—if your theory is correct, does it mean we might have a way to kill the entity?"

"It's possible." Sage glanced at the biohazard cooler that still contained samples of the entity. She had no desire to experiment further on them. She and her friends had already taken enough chances today.

"The problem is its defense mechanism. We have to figure out a way to deliver an acidic compound without needing to make contact again. And then figure out how to do it for the whole ship, section by section."

"Right. What could we use?"

"I'm thinking, we stick with chlorine. We use it as a disinfectant cleaner and as a water purifier for the pools and in water recycling so, by my reckoning, we'll have enough of the stuff. We'd need to convert it into a gas to deliver it, then add it to water to make it lethal."

"How does that work?"

"Well, it creates hydrochloric acid. As the entity

defends itself against us, the gas is our only way to reach it without being harmed. If we use the fire suppression system to spray a mist of water into all those areas where the gas has been delivered, we create an acidic solution that should work."

"Okay. How do we create the gas?"

"We can use the hydrochloric acid we have here in the lab. But chlorine gas is dangerous to us. It liquifies human lung tissue and causes serious burns to exposed soft tissue."

"We'll have to seal the safe zones completely to avoid the gas escaping into them."

"Noah, that thing has caused a lot of damage to the ship's ventilation system. How can we be certain the safe zones will be airtight?" Sage worried about the unintended consequences of their plan. "If the chlorine gas leaks into the safe zones, it could kill a lot of people." For the first time that day, she thought about her elderly mother and her sister, Rose. She hadn't seen them in over a week and guilty tears blurred her vision.

"Positive pressure?" Noah's suggestion brought her out of her thoughts. "We increase the air pressure in the safe zones. It will hold the gas out."

"It will. The system will have to stay stable for a fairly lengthy period while we gas the entity and then—

" she stopped, stricken.

"Sage, what is it?"

"Noah, did you hear what I just said? We're going to *kill* this thing. With gas. Like . . . like the Nazis killed all those people that time."

Sage had a hard time reconciling the line they had just crossed.

"We're creating a plan to actively extinguish this thing's life."

"We have to," Noah said quietly.

"I know. It's just . . . it's a newly-discovered life form and we're sworn to uphold the Treaty for the Protection and Preservation of Non-Human Life Forms."

"Sage, it's us, or it's the entity. It's a matter of self-defense—survival. We have to do it." Noah rested a hand on her shoulder and she lifted her chin to meet his gaze. He looked sad but determined.

It was then that she spotted a bruised lump on the side of his neck. Sage's eyes scanned the area before shooting back to his. He moved to step away from her and she grabbed his hand.

"Noah, is that from—?"

He nodded. "It doesn't matter. I don't want you to worry about me right now. We have to get the plan done and the gas deployed."

"Seriously?" She stared daggers at him, her mouth agape. "Were you *really not going to tell me* you got a piece of that thing stuck in your neck?"

He could have told her. She could have dug it out.

"You wouldn't have been able to," Noah said as if reading her thoughts.

"How do you know?"

"Because I tried." He sighed. "It dug itself in deeper and sent out splinters. Just like the big spike."

"My God! Noah." She collapsed onto her chair, stunned and sick to her stomach. "You're as good as dead . . ." her voice trailed off as her mind completed that thought. *And you will die horribly—just like Trigg did.*

Tears flowed down her cheeks and she tried to say how sorry she was. Nothing but a loud hiccup and gulp came out and then she burst into sobs.

Noah tugged her into a gentle embrace. "Jesus, Sage. I'm not dead yet." He tried to sound brave, but his voice cracked.

"Oh, Noah—I'm so sorry. We should have been more careful. We should have been wearing hazmat suits."

"I realized that afterwards, but by then there was no point bringing it up. The shard was already in my neck."

She glowered at him. "Don't you be like that. We can still beat this thing. We can get it out of you. We have time." Sage scanned the tabletop for a scalpel.

"The ship is our first priority. Captain's orders, Sage. If we get done exterminating our invader, you can take a look at the shard in my neck."

"I've copied all of my research and the videos onto the central database. When Mara comes in, she and a team can start working on a cure for you and anyone else who's infected." Sage sniffed, recovering her resolve and ignoring Noah's resignation. His condition had started a countdown for her. She was determined to do everything to save him.

Noah's device pinged. "They're expecting me back in Engineering soon. There's an update due on what the ship-wide levels of infestation look like. I'll fill Bo in on the progress you've made here with the chlorine and we can get to work on determining the quantities of the chemicals we need to do a ship-wide disbursement."

Sage nodded. She looked at the biohazard cooler and the petri dishes laid out on the bench in front of it. She reached for a sample dish.

"Before you go, I want to try the chlorine. It will be useful to know how quickly the entity defends itself, and also how long it takes for our solution to kill it." She was no longer concerned about the death of the crystalline life form. Everything had changed the moment she knew it had taken her best friend hostage.

She took a petri dish to the fume cupboard where she carefully removed the lid. With a final look at Noah to see that he was well back from the experiment, she added a few drops of liquid calcium hypochlorite to a beaker and added the acid to a siphon. She set the timer on the siphon to deliver the acid to the beaker in thirty seconds. Sage stepped back, closed the cupboard doors and focused on the screen showing the inside of the fume cupboard.

The timer counted down and when it hit zero seconds, the siphon released the acid which mixed with the calcium hypochlorite. A vapor began to form in the cupboard. Sage punched in the instructions for a fine jet of water to be released into the cabinet. Within seconds, tiny shards shot off the crystalline mass, embedding in the sides and roof of the enclosed space. Then, after less than a minute, the whole structure began to dissolve, bubbling and steaming as it turned into a cloudy liquid. The solution had worked. She stared at the puddle in the petri dish, waiting.

"How will we know if it's dead?"

"Poke it," said Noah.

"Jesus, you're brave."

"I have nothing to lose, remember?"

His words stole Sage's ability to speak for a moment. She vented the fume cupboard and, wearing a thick silicon glove, picked up a lab spoon. She carefully opened an arm hole on the side of the cupboard and with shaky fingers, gave the dish of liquid a poke.

Nothing.

She stirred it.

Still nothing.

Her courage grew and she carefully lifted the dish out of the fume cupboard, covered it with the lid and gave it a vigorous shake.

The bubbles settled and the liquid remained inert. There was no reaction.

"Let's take a closer look."

She held the dish at arm's length and walked back to the bench. She carefully removed the lid and drew some liquid up into a pipette and sandwiched a thin drop between two glass slides. Sage clicked the slides into place under the microscope and focused the eyepieces.

"The lattice is completely broken down. There's no activity at all. It worked. There's no evidence of anything other than dissolved minerals. If there was something making the mass samples sentient, it's not here now. The crystals have dissolved, and the solution is now water. That cloudy residue is probably calcium chloride."

"That's good news, right?"

"Yes. This is a good way to eliminate the entity. It's a pity we have to do it before we figure out how sentient, and or, intelligent the crystal mass is." As a scientist, Sage found the discovery intriguing. The destruction of the entity would be a lost opportunity to learn more about it, but there was no other way, and she made her peace with their decision.

"I've got to go. Are you okay here by yourself for a bit?"

"Yes. I'll work on the pressurization model for containment. Meanwhile, Engineering needs to get some ventilation systems back online to achieve a positive-pressure curtain. Otherwise, you should also check that the fire suppression system is functioning optimally. We need the water spray to create the hydrochloric acid from the gas." Sage sat, fighting exhaustion. It had been a tough day. She rubbed her temple.

"You okay?" Noah said.

Her eyes welled with tears. She shook her head,

buried her face against his chest, and hugged him tightly. He could be dead in a few hours, and her heart ached. Why had she not realized sooner what he really meant to her? She'd used all her energy and time fighting the system, determined not to sink comfortably into the predictable life laid before her. Why had she been so myopic as to miss the opportunity to love and be loved in return?

She lifted her face and met his haunted gaze.

Sounding resigned, he said, "Sage, I know we've been friends forever, and it will be hard. But you have Dylan. I saw the way he looked at you. You'll forget about me soon enough."

"No, I won't! I think I—" Sage's voice snagged on a painful lump in her throat. She couldn't say it. She couldn't even whisper the words she'd only now discovered she wanted to say.

"God, woman, your timing really sucks, but it's okay. It will be okay." Noah's voice cracked and he rested his forehead against hers for a moment. He started to straighten up when she reached for his face with both hands.

"I know I'm not the most likable person. And I'm a fool for only figuring out now what you mean to me. I've always thought no one could love me, so I never examined my own feelings. But I think I love you. I think I have for a long time. I don't want you to die."

Her shuddering, tear-soaked confession broke the silence in the lab. Slowly, and with great tenderness, Noah kissed her.

"Well, if you think you're unlovable, you're wrong. You've had me from the start, I was just too stubborn to give in to it. I'm sorry."

A chasm of sorrow engulfed Sage when he left the lab. Her mind raged at the unfairness of fate. An appalling shadow hung over her. They'd discovered new life only to realize they had to kill it to survive its all-consuming attack on them. With the imminent loss of Noah approaching, Sage's victory over the entity would be a hollow one.

ELEVEN

Time log: Day: 36,136. Hour: 20:25

"Dylan, can you hear me?"

"Sorry, Sage, our bridge comms are shorting out. The entity—it's reached this level and it's moving quickly."

"Oh, my God! Is everyone all right?" The bustle of Engineering made it hard to hear him over the poor connection. She had arrived there only minutes earlier and was immediately assigned the task of reestablishing contact with the bridge.

"So far. I can't figure out how, but it *knows* that the controls of the ship are here. I have a really bad feel—"

Static hissed. His voice cut off and Sage swallowed.

"Dylan?" *What do I do?* "Dylan!" Taking a deep breath, she gathered her thoughts. Isolating the entity and driving it back from the bridge was a priority.

We can't lose control of the bridge. Without the bridge, we'll have no flight controls, no communication and no hope.

What could she do to buy the crew up there some time?

Hazmat suits!

If she could get suits up to Dylan, the bridge crew stood a better chance of holding out until the evacuation and extermination could clear their section.

"I'm going back to the lab to get suits for the bridge personnel."

"You need help?" Noah asked.

"I'll get someone there to help me. You guys have your hands full."

It was the truth. Engineering was a hive of activity, every available technician, engineer and apprentice was on duty to help get the chlorine solution prepared and the drums in place to deploy the extermination plan. Time-release valves were connected to the central system and the execution would all take place well back from the active zone.

Sage raced back to the Sciences lab, skidding to a stop when the doors only slid partially open. She peered in, and it took a moment to grasp the scene inside. She stepped sideways through the opening and watched, silently confused. Mara and several other lab technicians were calmly smashing lab equipment with their bare hands. They moved slowly, their expressions blank, showing zero emotion. There was blood everywhere; smeared on counters and pooling on the floor. They didn't cry out when broken glass cut their hands or hit their faces.

Sage knew instantly she was in danger.

She took one, then two steps back, and felt for the door access panel, unwilling to take her eyes off the systematic destruction. She reached back, and her hand slid over smooth, warm hardness. The control panel was covered with crystalline crust that was growing rapidly. She recoiled, terrified. Was she trapped?

She uttered a barely audible moan that seemed to echo in the sudden stillness. Her eyes grew wide, her nerves primed. She spun slowly around.

The lab workers had halted their rampage and were staring at her. Their glittering, lemon-yellow eyes filled her with dread. Confused and unwilling to believe what she was seeing, she took a step forward to ask Mara what had happened to them. Her supervisor lurched towards her. Sage jumped at the unnatural movement. The rest of the workers did the same thing. Realization dawned. Somehow, the entity was controlling them. The half-dead stares of her co-workers snapped her out of her stupor. She sucked in a ragged breath and gagged on the metallic odor of blood.

Think! You need a way out, Sage.

She searched the shelves for anything she could use to open the doors and spotted a huge dark-brown bottle. It was difficult to move, but she dragged it off its shelf. Her hands trembled and she almost dropped it before she put it down with a thud at her feet. She twisted the heavy cap, lifted the bottle in both hands and tossed an oily splash of sulfuric acid at the control panel.

A collective shriek issued from the lab workers who stopped suddenly, surprise twisting their already-grotesque features. Bunches of crystal protrusions bloomed from their necks and bodies. Their screams faded as some of them dropped to the floor and transformed the same way as Trigg had.

Her panic rose but Sage focused on the access panel. The acid had worked. The crust over the controls had turned white and chalky. She capped the bottle, ignoring the painful acid burns on her fingers. She smashed at the dead crystal with a covered fist and cleared the panel, hitting the open button hard. The doors slid a few centimeters apart then stopped.

"Damn!" She rested the bottle next to her feet and grabbed each door and pulled. She glanced over her shoulder when the scrape and shuffle of the crystallizing lab workers got closer. The ones that hadn't transformed yet were intent on stopping her escape.

"Jesus, motherfu—" The one door budged an inch and Sage leaned in, shoving them apart with all her might. "Argh!"

The doors opened enough for her to step sideways through the narrow gap. She reached back to retrieve the sulfuric acid and a bloodied hand touched her arm. It jerked back just as suddenly, her skin still dotted with drops of viscous acid.

Sage hefted the brown bottle up and fled back towards Engineering. She only stopped when she was through another set of doors that she could close and lock.

Pain radiated up her arms and she hazarded a look at her hands. They were covered in burns. When she'd splashed the control panel, some acid had messed down the outside of the bottle. She had it all over her. Holes were burned through her sleeves and shirtfront from hugging the bottle of acid to her body as she fled the lab.

Gasping for breath, and still running on adrenalin, Sage lifted the bottle again and staggered across the concourse. It was almost deserted. She quickened her pace, unwilling to have another dreadful encounter with people infected by the entity. Praying silently, she worried for the safety of her family who were in the first evacuation wave that had been sent to the far end of the ship. The idea of more people becoming unwilling hosts to the entity sickened her and she shoved the thought aside, focusing on getting to the secure confines of Engineering.

The noisy bustle when she arrived soothed her ragged nerves. Sage set the bottle down slowly onto the floor and collapsed in a winded heap into a chair close to Noah's workstation.

"Sage! What happened?" Noah rushed over and crouched next to her, examining her hands.

"The lab. I can't explain it, but it looked as if the entity took control of the lab workers. Some of them died like . . . Trigg. Others seemed single-minded in their pursuit of me." She swallowed, and gratefully accepted a glass of water. "I got away because I splashed acid on the crust over the access controls. It burned my hands." She looked at the fiery red sores and her bloody fingers.

"Someone, get me a first aid kit."

A kit was deposited next to him and Noah rummaged through it.

"I don't understand how some people are controlled

and others die so quickly, and you . . ." Sage paused, not sure how to say it.

"You're wondering why I'm still walking, talking, and breathing? Me, too. Trust me. It's crossed my mind." He sighed. "Only thing I can think of, is the fragment that hit me must have been tiny. Like a fine splinter."

"And, perhaps, the others have been infected with larger pieces. That might explain how you're still alive. I'm still curious about the control. I wonder how it's doing that," Sage said, mystified by the entity and its behavior.

"Adaptation. I think that from the time it took Trigg, it's become bolder in how it perceives us. This thing is smart. Smarter than us."

"That seems obvious now. It evaded our detection systems, is making us host organisms, and is systematically destroying our ability to defend ourselves. That lab was a wreck. Without the science, we have little to no insight into it." Sage was thoughtful as Noah dressed her wounded hands.

"Exactly. The experiment you did in the lab is probably the reason that area was targeted."

"Those poor people."

"I'm just glad we came up with a solution before it could stop us. I'm sorry about the scientists. It's a huge loss, but at least we have what we need to save everyone else." Noah sat back on his heels, done with the first aid to her burns.

Sage looked at his neck, trying to hide her horror. The blossoming crystals pushed through the skin, turning it shades of blue and black. Noah caught her attention and she raised a brow, still a little stunned by yet another narrow escape.

"Is that the acid?" He nodded at the glass bottle.

"Yes. Sulfuric. It was on a shelf near the door."

"Quick thinking. Did it work the way you wanted it to?"

"I wouldn't be here if it hadn't. That access panel was covered, this thick"—she held two fingers a few centimeters apart—"in crystal mass before I splashed it and broke away the dead bits."

"You're brave. And I'm glad you're okay."

"How are you doing?" Sage glanced again at the bruising on Noah's neck. His face was pale and he looked to be in considerable pain himself.

"Okay for now. I'm still able to do my part in this fight."

"Maybe we can—"

"Maybe we need to get back to work, Sage." Noah rose, cleared his throat and waited for her to get up.

"We've made more progress on the delivery of the chlorine gas and we've confirmed that we have a sufficient supply to get to a deadly saturation level on each deck. The fire suppression system is online and primed."

"That's good. Where do we start?" She tried to ignore his evasive change of topic.

"The aft sections. That's where the greatest concentration of infestation has occurred because of the asteroid strike between decks six and eight."

"Lucky for us that it struck in the cargo holds, I suppose." She felt little relief from the report, but it was something. At least the asteroid hadn't struck them midships or closer to the bow. The greatest concentration of people and greenhouses was in the forward half of the vessel.

"I suppose it's lucky. The evacuation to the forward section is almost done and we'll be able to seal the containment doors in twenty minutes. Then we pump the gas in through every open vent, grate, drain and inlet we have beyond that barrier."

"How long to do that?"

"About an hour to reach maximum concentration and spray the water," Noah said. "After that we need to work quickly to vent and clean the aft section to clear any remaining pockets of gas and flush the acid. The acid's going to be corrosive, damaging equipment and structures, but if we're fast, destruction should be minimal. After that we'll repeat the whole procedure in the bow when we've evacuated everyone and moved everything we can. The greenhouses are being harvested and the seed bank and grow stations are being prepped for moving. We'll lose some stuff for sure and it will take time to recover."

Sage nodded, regretting the inevitable damage and the loss of the greenhouses.

"Any idea of how many people have been . . . you know?" She glanced at his neck and Noah reached up to rub it self-consciously.

"From your report, we're assuming most of the Science department. Then there were a few workers in the aft section, and we've heard nothing from the bridge for a while."

"Damn. We'll have to isolate anyone still alive and figure out how to treat them."

She missed the hard look Noah gave her.

"That's the medical team's issue. We have enough on our plates just getting that thing to let go of the ship."

"You're right." She focused her attention on the job

at hand. "Okay. How do we stop it from reestablishing itself in the aft section?"

"Guards will be posted at the only unsealed entry points. They'll be armed with acid solutions. Other than that, we maintain the positive pressure curtain and drop the ship's temperatures right down."

"Oh."

"Yeah, it's going to get really cold in here soon." Noah spoke fast and worked his device. Time was not on their side.

A flash of memory pricked at her and she exclaimed, "You said the bridge was infected?"

"Possibly."

"I almost forgot I was talking with Dylan right before I went to the lab. I wasn't able to retrieve the hazmat suits! I was preoccupied with fighting my way out of there." She swallowed, dreading her next words. "You said you haven't heard anything more from them. I wonder if they're okay."

He grimaced at her.

"Noah, what is it?"

He seemed to war with himself over what to tell her and she crossed her arms. "Tell me now, or I swear I'll—"

"The ship appears to be losing power. We're maybe

off course too. I can't confirm any of this, but it's not looking good, Sage."

She stared at him, lost for words. Their situation became more dire the longer the entity held the *Vega Four* captive. It was tempting to be pessimistic, but she reached deep into her reserves of courage.

"It's time we took back control. This thing has to go. And soon. Where's Bo?" she asked as she looked around the room for the chief engineer.

Buried behind a stack of status reports, studying a holographic layout of the aft cargo holds, Bo looked up when Noah and Sage approached his workstation.

"Bo, are we close to triggering the extermination?" Noah asked.

"Close, but not quite there. We're missing the captain's sign-off."

"Bo, if you wait for the sign-off, we're all dead," Sage said, glancing from the chief to Noah. "From what Dylan told me earlier, and the fact that you haven't been able to reach them again, we must assume the bridge is under attack. That means you're the highest-ranking officer available to make the call."

"I understand you're anxious to get this operation moving, but until we know the captain and the bridge crew are out of commission, we can't move. It's a Code

Thirteen violation. I have orders—"

"Bo, people are dying in gruesome ways. I've seen it with my own eyes. Please! Let's do this."

He sighed and shook his head. His determination not to break rank drove her mad.

"God, you can't be serious?" she yelled.

"I am. We need to be certain the chain of command is broken before I assume—"

"Bo."

Everyone turned to stare at Dylan Gray. He looked worse for wear, but he was alive.

"Dylan, thank God." Sage smiled with relief. He returned her smile, but a darkness haunted his expression.

"The pilot and I are the only ones left."

"Jesus." Noah looked shocked. The room fell into a momentary silence as the news of the bridge crew's fate spread.

"I guess that means I'm in charge, and I say let's go get that fucking monster," Dylan hissed through clenched teeth.

Sage's gaze slid to Bo and he nodded, a sneer twisting his lips. "Let's do it," he said.

The order galvanized the engineering crew and the cramped control room buzzed with noisy tension as they prepared to lock down the aft sections. Final checks were completed and controllers turned to their commanders for further orders.

"Enter the codes," Bo said.

The containment doors were armed, isolating the aft section. Bo straightened, stepped back and nodded to Dylan to execute the final command.

Dylan, weary but alert, hesitated then pressed his finger down firmly on the control panel. An alarm sounded and the screens and monitors turned to orange and black. The high alert phase would remain in place until after their operation, when the ship was secured.

"Activate the chlorine gas inflow."

Sage and the others watched the blueprint of the aft section on the screen. The air quality overlay gradually changed from blue, to yellow, to red.

"Approaching one hundred percent chlorine gas saturation," said the controller handling the gas delivery.

The blueprint blinked once then remained red.

"Saturation levels reached, sir."

"Good. Activate the fire suppression system."

"Fire suppression system is active and delivering, sir."

The clock blinked at them as the seconds passed.

How much time would the acid need to kill the entity? No one knew exactly, but they had to find the balance between the delivery and the destruction of the ship. Sage had guessed no more than three minutes would be needed and as the timer approached that moment, the room hummed with stress.

"Vent the atmosphere and activate the fire suppression system again to wash the acid away." Bo's instructions were calm. His tone belied the tension in the room.

"Yes, sir."

They waited, anxious and hopeful. Time seemed to slow down for Sage. She was lost in thought when Noah winced and sank into a chair next to her.

"Noah?"

"This thing is really hurting all of a sudden. Damn." He put a shaky hand to his neck and touched the bruising gingerly. When he drew his fingers away, they were covered in blood.

"Oh, Noah. I wish this wasn't happening." Sage took his other hand and hugged it to her chest. Tears filled her eyes. She was helpless to stem his pain.

His breathing was shallow and he winced again then groaned.

"Is he okay?" Dylan came over. His eyes widened

when he spied the glinting protrusion from Noah's neck. "Jesus Christ, Sage!"

"It's from when we were trying to get our video proof for Captain Ellis." Sorrow made it difficult for her to speak.

"God. I'm sorry. We should have been more careful." Dylan crouched next to Noah, his concern obvious.

"Sir, we have a problem."

Dylan rose and strode over to the controller's desk. "What is it?"

"The controls for venting of the atmosphere are not responding. I've tried twice to initiate the purge and cleanse but nothing's working."

"There's a manual override," Bo said hanging his head.

"Yes, but—"

The controller stared at Bo, then at Dylan.

"What?" Dylan asked.

"It's on the control panel on the other side of the containment doors," said Noah. His voice was weak and thin.

"Shit. Now what?" Bo ran his hand over his head.

"I'll go." Noah rose on shaky legs.

"No. No way. That's suicide!" Sage yelled.

"It's the only way we'll be able to finish the operation."

"No, you can't . . ." Her voice failed and she shook her head.

"Noah," Dylan approached him and put a hand on his shoulder, "are you sure?"

"I'm dead anyway, Dylan. I might as well make it count for something, right?" He looked around the room. Every set of eyes was trained on him, despair on all the faces.

"No." Sage gulped. "NO!" She launched herself at Noah and clung to him.

He hugged her gently for a moment then pried her arms loose and pushed her back. Dylan took her and held her close. She couldn't believe what Noah planned to do.

"If you're going to do it, you'll need to go now," Bo said in a bleak tone.

Noah nodded, winced and looked at Sage again. He touched her wet cheek and turned to go.

"I'm going down there with you," she said. "I'll stay on the other side of the containment doors. I'm not leaving you to die alone." A tear rolled down his cheek, but he said nothing.

"I'll come too. We'll be safer in a group." Dylan

grabbed his jacket and one for Sage. The air in Engineering had become frigid. The corridors would be much colder.

"Let's go."

Noah led the way. Sage pulled on the heavy coat and tucked her injured hand gently into his. As they walked, she kept glancing up at him. His condition seemed to deteriorate with every step. How much time did he have left until the deadly blossoming occurred? She pushed the awful thought away to savor her last moments with him.

"Take this." Dylan handed Sage a full facemask, complete with rebreather. "There might be some gas leakage when Noah goes into the containment zone. We'll stay well clear of the entrance. The masks are just in case."

She numbly accepted the bulky equipment.

They walked on in silence until they reached a set of heavy metal doors. The doors were frosty but free of crystalline growths.

"Okay, Noah. I'll ask you again, are you sure you want to do this?"

"I am." His reply was a hoarse whisper and Dylan grimaced and held out a mask for him.

"No. It will only prolong . . . this." His energy

waned.

"It's been an honor to serve with you," Dylan said and reached out to shake Noah's hand. "On behalf of the crew and the passengers of the *Vega Four,* we are grateful for your sacrifice. You will not be forgotten, Noah."

Sage whimpered and the men both turned as she wiped her face. It was useless. More tears wet her cheeks the moment she cleared the last ones.

"Goodbye, Sage. I hope you don't miss me too much." Noah embraced her tenderly and kissed her forehead. He looked at Dylan and said, "Look after her."

"I will. I promise." Dylan gathered Sage under his arm and the two of them retreated. "Open the doors," he said into his comms link.

Noah coughed, then quickly slipped inside when a gap opened. The containment doors slammed closed and Sage lost sight of him.

"Noah!" She raced for the doors. The hint of chlorine that had wafted through the opening stung her eyes. She coughed and a second later, Dylan was there, pulling her mask over her face and turning it on. Her breathing eased and she turned to peer through the tiny window above the door control panel.

She could see Noah on his knees on the other

side of the thick glass. He coughed and his face had turned red, his eyes streaming from the combination of chlorine and acid still lingering in the air.

"Get up, Noah. Please get up." Her voice was muffled inside the mask.

He finally managed to stand again and staggered back against the control panel near the door. Blood streaked the wall. His hands looked burned and he was clearly suffering.

"Oh God, Dylan. Why did we let him to do this?" Sage's torment at watching her beloved friend suffer overwhelmed her, and she wept. Dylan rubbed her shoulders to offer some comfort. It was useless. Nothing could ease the trauma of witnessing Noah's agonizing final moments.

He activated the control panel, punched in the codes on the eroded panel and stopped right before he was about to execute the purge. She wanted his suffering to end. Why had he stopped?

The answer came when the back of his shirt split open and dark, blood-streaked crystals emerged from beneath his skin.

Sage screamed, falling back against Dylan. Neither of them could bring themselves to look away.

Noah reached for the control panel with a

trembling and bloody hand and hit the flickering yellow command button at last. The alarm sounded and a forceful vacuum pulled at him. His hair and shredded shirt whipped in the stiff wind of departing air. The evacuating atmosphere whistled at the tiny spaces around the doors and built to a keening howl. The massive doors vibrated but held.

Noah braced against the wind and glanced back at the control window. He smiled and Sage watched his pained expression change to relief. He let go of the handle he'd been clinging to and disappeared from view.

Sage shut her eyes tight and tried not to imagine his final journey into the cold vacuum of space.

"Bo?" Dylan's voice cracked.

"I read you."

"Start the cleanse. The vent is complete."

"Copy that. Cleanse initiated." Bo's voice over the comms link sounded sad.

"Come on. We should head back," Dylan said to Sage who had taken off the mask to wipe uselessly at the endless flow of tears.

They trudged away from the ice-covered containment doors in an eerie silence. Sage stiffened, awareness causing gooseflesh to rise on her arms and neck. For the first time since it had invaded, the entity was still. The groans, which had accompanied its spread as it had overwhelmed corridors and breached walls and doors, had stopped. The air in the zone in which the entity still existed began to crackle with electric tension.

"Do you hear that?" she asked.

Dylan stopped and frowned at her. "Is that a good sign or an omen of worse things to come?"

They got their answer a moment later when the stillness was split by a throbbing shriek that hurt their ears.

"Run. Back to Engineering. Run!" Dylan shoved Sage forward and the two of them hurtled for the safety of the engineering complex.

The corridors erupted with spikes and jagged growths. The air felt alive around them. They ran faster, trying to stay ahead of the razor-sharp protrusions chasing after them.

At the entrance to Engineering, Dylan yelled, "Spray it. Now!"

Six crew members in hazmat suits stepped forward, carrying canisters filled with an acid solution. They opened the hoses up and doused the approaching crystal growths. The spears and shafts froze and turned white, bubbling and releasing harmless gas clouds as they died. Some crumbled, others merely atrophied.

Sage gasped for breath, holding her stomach. Then she fell to her knees and sobbed. Their flight back to Engineering had momentarily distracted her from her grief. Now, wave after wave of sorrow coursed through her.

He was gone.

"Clear the aft section. Deploy the robot cleaners and let's get people moving. Quick as you can, please." Dylan had regained his composure and took command of the situation.

People ran, others worked their control panels with laser-focus. Sage sat in a heap on the floor, numb and exhausted as the activity to save the ship continued around her.

TWELVE

Time log: Day: 36,136. Hour: 23:47

Hours had passed. Sage had no idea how many.

Her stomach growled and pins-and-needles pricked her left foot. She got up, sagged into a chair, and laying her head on her arms, stared at Dylan and Bo who had emerged from a short meeting with Engineering's head controllers.

"Right. Deck by deck evacuations starting at Deck One. Move everyone to beyond the containment doors and secure your section. Go." Dylan's command was followed by organized chaos. Lights flashed and comms messages flew. The evacuation shifted the entire population of the ship and all the plant life they were able to carry, into the aft section that had been cleansed earlier.

"Right, let's go, everyone." Bo gave the order to evacuate Engineering to the secondary engineering control room in the aft section on Deck Four.

"Come on, Sage." Dylan helped her to her feet.

They moved carefully, the ship a maze of glinting, crystalline barbs that positively vibrated with hostility. Sage tried to ignore it.

"Dylan, do you know how many crew and passengers have been infected?"

"More than a third, from our final count."

"So many?" Sage was stunned. How would they recover from the losses? "My family," she murmured, but no one heard her in the din of movement and voices.

Sometime later, they had taken up station on Deck Four and the same procedure that had cleared the aft section was initiated.

"Containment doors are secure, Commander." A controller looked at Dylan, waiting on his orders.

"Deploy the chlorine gas."

"Yes, sir."

The gas saturation levels were reached and the tension in the room grew.

"Initiate the fire suppression system."

"Fire suppression system delivering, sir."

They waited the requisite amount of time then Dylan said in an emotionless voice. "Proceed with atmosphere venting."

To everyone's relief, the second atmospheric purge went without any problems.

"Purge is complete, sir. Proceeding with cleanse."

"Good work, everyone." Dylan slumped into a corroded metal chair next to Sage and closed his eyes. "I can't remember the last time I ate something, but I am not even remotely hungry," he mumbled.

"Same. I doubt I could eat anything after what I've seen this past two days."

He grunted and Sage turned to look at him. He had dark shadows under his eyes and his face was dirty.

"You could use a shower before your induction."

"What?"

"You're the highest-ranking officer here, besides Bo. That makes you our new captain, Dylan."

"Shit."

"That reminds me, can you please leave the etiquette AI turned off? That thing was so full of crap."

Dylan smiled at the small joke and then got up to check their progress. He and Bo huddled together over the controls.

Sage felt empty. Their victory had come at great cost. She felt like a different person to the one who had woken this morning, full of bluster and rebellion. The nightmare had changed her.

More than at any other time in her life, she felt an affinity for the people around her. They were all survivors of a terrible attack. The ship, and each person left standing, faced an uncertain future. But, whereas she used to feel confined and imprisoned, she now felt connected to the ship, bonded to it, and to the people around her.

It had taken the crystalline entity's invasion for her to appreciate the vessel they occupied, that carried them through the depths of space. It no longer felt like a prison, but like a womb. They were the progeny of generations of people before them, and the forebears of an, as yet, untold story. The *Vega Four* was their mother. Sage would never again take for granted the privilege of being one of the few to live aboard a generation ship bound for a distant galaxy.

She went to a window and peered into the blackness beyond. She finally felt at home in space. It was time to start living her life. So much of it had already been wasted by fighting her fate.

Noah was gone. She would never have that time with him back and her regret and guilt would be constant reminders of all that was lost in this fight. With a silent promise to the blackness that was now his eternal home, she vowed to live a better life.

"The damage is significant," Bo said. "The *Vega Four* will not be able to sustain us for much more than a few weeks. Two months, tops."

"I started a distress signal from the bridge before I escaped to Engineering," Dylan said. "The other *Vega* ships should be receiving it by tomorrow." He rubbed his face and shook his head. They'd done everything they could. He stood behind Sage and placed a warm hand on her shoulder.

"I promise. We'll honor him somehow."

"Thank you," she said. Her thoughts had, indeed, drifted to Noah again. "He was so brave."

"Yes, he was. Come on. Let's get some rest. Tomorrow is going to be a busy day."

"Do you regret that we had to kill the entity in order to survive?" Sage asked.

"I do. I think it would have been incredible to communicate with it, to try and understand what it needed or wanted. Given that chance, we may have been able to prevent its destruction and much of the damage to the ship. We could have saved lives had there been enough time to learn more about what we were dealing with."

"I agree. We'll have to live with our choice."

"Under the circumstances, it was our only choice. We have a responsibility to every living thing on this ship to keep the *Vega Four* safe. In a way, we failed.

We'll have to evacuate the ship when help arrives. But in other ways, we were victorious. We saved the majority of people and plants." He sighed and added after a brief pause, "We can hope that the entity exists somewhere else out there. There's always a chance that the asteroid was not its only home."

"We can hope."

"We can also hope we never come across it again."

"I second that."

They walked away to find somewhere to rest. It would be a rough night of sleeping on floors and under tables, but they would all wake up to a fresh start in a vast universe filled with endless possibilities.

Dear Reader,

Thank you for reading **A Dark Genesis**. I hope you enjoyed this novella. Please remember that authors rely on reviews and every reader that leaves one is helping other readers choose the books they will enjoy. I hope you review **A Dark Genesis** where you purchased it and on Goodreads.com

More to follow in the **Journey to Vega** story series.

Cheryl Lawson,
Author

More from Cheryl Lawson.

The Rubicon Saga books: **We Are Mars, Storm At Dawn, Break the Dark.**

Series description: Mars is home to Rubicon, an intrepid science mission made up of two factions—g-mods and non-gens. Tensions run high across the class divide, but their petty disagreements soon pale into insignificance when they're faced with a series of disturbing and deadly disasters and challenges.

Separating the weak from the strong; the brave from the timid and the loyal Mars settlers from the traitors, forces beyond their control test the bonds of love, friendship and duty. Get swept along with Dana, Jaxon, Lenny, Chuck, Zane, Swift and Toni as they traverse the unforgiving Mars landscape, dive deep into its underground labyrinths and fight for their survival against the odds, and against enemies known and unknown.

We Are Mars, Storm At Dawn and Break the Dark are the epic and thrilling books of the **Rubicon Saga.** Each story brings you adventure, excitement, intrigue, romance and a cast of incredible characters who must fight to survive, to live and love on a far off and hostile world.

Available in ebook and paperback from book sellers, including Amazon.

FIND Cheryl online at:

Website: **cheryllawson.net**

Instagram: **cheryl_lawson_**

Threads: **cheryl_lawson_**

Goodreads: search **Cheryl Lawson**

Acknowledgements

Thank you to my beta readers who helped immeasurably in developing this story. A big thanks to Crystal L. Kirkham for editing A Dark Genesis. A special thanks to David who's endless support and encouragement are the reasons why this book even exists. Your support means the world to me.

And lastly, thank you readers for enjoying my stories and supporting my journey as an author.

Cheryl